THE FOUNDLING IN THE FLOWERS

THE AMISH QUILTING CIRCLE

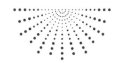

SARAH MILLER

IRENE GLICK

SWEETBOOKHUB.COM

WELCOME TO THE AMISH QUILTING CIRCLE

What is more lovely than a quilting circle? Where, good friends can come together to drink coffee, eat cake, talk, and work on a quilt or two. It is a wonderful way to spend an afternoon being both productive and having fun.

Only, this quilting circle likes to do a little matchmaking along with the quilting.

Join the ladies of Faith's Creek as they see who they will match next.

All the books are sweet and family-friendly with no nasty surprises.

If you missed the first book, you can grab An Englischer's Folly or the rest of the books here.

If you are not already a member of my reader's newsletter, join here, for free, to be the first to find out when new books are released and for occasional free content.

CHAPTER ONE

FAITH'S CREEK, PENNSYLVANIA

*T*he scent of the flowers was intoxicating. Every shade and color was there in all *Gott's* glory – golden asters, pink begonias, yellow tulips, red carnations, orange gerberas, bunches of silvery gypsophila, white lilies, purple verbena.

Annie Lapp breathed in and looked proudly around the flower store with a huge smile on her face. This had been her dream – a store of her own, selling cut flowers – and now that dream had come true. Annie hummed to herself, selecting flowers from this vase and that, holding them up into a bouquet, deciding which went best with which. Oh, there were so many combinations and she took her time in trying out different combinations.

This was to be a bouquet for an anniversary, and the gentleman had asked for his *fraa's* favorite color – pink – to feature prominently.

"I think some peonies would work well," she said out loud, just as the bell above the store door dinged. Annie turned to find Sarah Beiler – the bishop's *fraa* – entering the store.

"*Gut* morning, Annie – what a beautiful scent. It lifts your spirits, doesn't it?" Sarah said.

Annie knew her smile had grown even wider, if that was possible.

"*Gut* morning – it really does, doesn't it? When I open the door each morning, it's like I'm walking into the garden of Eden itself," she replied.

"And we all need our little piece of Eden, don't we? How long have you been open for now? Three months, is it? I don't know where the time goes," Sarah said.

"Three months last Monday. I never thought I'd make it happen. But here I am, and I couldn't be happier,"

Annie said, laying down the bouquet and wiping her hands on a cloth behind the counter.

The last three months had gone by in a whirl. It had been exciting, but a learning curve, too. Before coming to Faith's Creek, Annie had never run her own business, nor had she lived away from the home in Oregon, in the Amish community where she had grown up. But the death of her *mamm* the previous year had made her think more about the kind of life she wanted, and with the small inheritance she had received, Annie had decided to take a chance and open the flower store she had always dreamed of. Business was blooming, in every way, and Annie couldn't have been happier.

"And we couldn't imagine Faith's Creek without you." Sarah approached the display and closing her eyes took in a breath. "Delightful. Everyone's talking about the store. Your flowers are so beautiful, and the arrangements you make are something else. I'd like some lilies today. I love fresh lilies – the scent of them perfumes the house, though they make Bishop Beiler sneeze," Sarah said, chuckling a little. "Only when they first come in, I wouldn't be that cruel." There was a twinkle in her eyes.

Annie took four lily stems from a vase in the window. "I can help with that. I'll cut the stamens off – the pollen

3

gets everywhere. That's probably what's doing it. It's a nightmare to get off your clothes, too," Annie said, and she snipped the stamens from the open flowers, before wrapping them in tissue paper for Sarah, who was now examining the display in the window.

"You've got so many beautiful flowers, Annie. You really have. I know a lot of my friends in the quilting circle are planning to order from you on special occasions," Sarah said.

Annie grinned as she handed over the lilies and took the payment. Sarah Beiler had been ever so kind in supporting the flower store. She had told everyone she met about it, and many of Annie's customers had spoken of the bishop's *fraa's* recommendation.

"That's so kind of you to say, *denke*. I've felt so welcome in Faith's Creek since I arrived here. Everyone told me it was a risk, but it was one I'm only too glad I took," Annie replied.

She had arrived in Faith's Creek with two suitcases and a dream, but Annie had always had faith that she was doing the right thing.

"Follow your heart, Annie, that's how *Gott* leads us through life. It's like a compass, but *Gott* wants you to find your own way with it," her *mamm* had once said, and those words had remained with Annie through the doubts and uncertainties of leaving Oregon behind.

"We're glad you took it, too. We're blessed to have you. Well, *gut* day to you, Annie. I'll probably pop in tomorrow. It's Susanna Bontrager's birthday on Saturday and I think she'd appreciate some flowers," Sarah said.

Annie bid her goodbye and returned to the anniversary bouquet. She chose roses to finish it, tying the stems with brown twine, and wrapping the flowers in delicate tissue paper. It looked very pretty, and she felt proud to be part of such a special celebration.

It was almost closing time, and having finished the bouquet, Annie topped up the water in all the vases, rearranging her window display, before closing the store for the evening and stepping out onto the market square. The flower store was opposite the mercantile store, and she could see one of the counter clerks rearranging tins of paint in the window. He was balancing precariously on a stepladder, and Annie feared he would fall at any moment.

And all for a tin of paint, she thought to herself, as the store clerk reached out to place the tin he was holding on top of a pyramid of different colors.

As he was doing so, he glanced out of the window, catching Annie's eye as she watched him. The ladder wobbled, and Annie gasped as the man steadied himself with an embarrassed look on his face. He was attractive – tall with black hair and a kindly face. But now he turned his attention back to the paint.

Annie smiled, shaking her head as she made her way across the road toward home. She rented a cottage from a man named Ezekiel Bride, who owned several properties in Faith's Creek. It was a pleasant dwelling place, just a short walk from the store – a cottage with a parlor, small kitchen, and a bedroom in the roof space, reached by a narrow flight of stairs. Annie was happy there. Arriving home, she let herself in, and the sound of purring filled the air. Within moments her cat, Maisy, was curling around her ankles.

"Oh, Maisy, have you missed me?" she asked, reaching down and picking up the cat, stroking her head as Maisy rubbed herself against Annie's neck.

The cat purred, and Annie set her down, glancing around the parlor to see everything was as she had left it. Maisy had a habit of knocking things over. But the vase Annie had placed on the table that morning, containing a bloom of yellow tulips, was as she had left it, all was well in her lovely home. What more could she ask for?

She settled down for a quiet evening. Annie was content. She had not had an easy life – her *daed* had died when she was very young, and her *mamm* had struggled to bring her up with only limited means. Annie missed her *mamm* terribly, but she knew she would be proud of her – she had her dream, and now she intended to live it as best she could.

"I'll see you later, Maisy. Be *gut* – there's milk in your saucer," Annie said, as she closed the door of the cottage the next morning.

She smiled to herself, imagining what others would think if they could hear her talking to the cat as though she were a real person.

You're turning into a cat lady, she thought to herself, shaking her head as she walked across the market square. *Nee,* she was just a lady with a cat. There had been some cruel boys in her old home. They had teased one of the spinsters. Saying she was sad and lonely and just a cat lady. The image of their faces stopped her for a moment.

She shook it off. She was not sad or old and she loved her cat. They were the hateful ones and should be ashamed.

Annie was only twenty-three years old, but she had always been a mature sort of person – practical and hardworking. Her *mamm* had instilled those qualities into her at an early age, and she took matters of business very seriously. Some in Oregon had told her a woman's place was not in running a flower store – or any business, for that matter. Finding a husband was what mattered, but those same people had now been proved wrong. Annie was proving herself successful, and she did not need a husband to validate her success. But despite this self-determination, there were times when Annie longed for companionship. She had worked so hard at building the business that her personal relationships had been neglected. She had acquaintances in Faith's Creek, but no one she could call a true friend.

"*Gut* morning, Annie," Monica Hertz, one of the stall-holders said, as Annie unlocked the door of the flower store.

Monica sold knitting supplies, and Annie wished her *gut* morning, before entering the store, where the heady scent of the flowers perfumed the air. She loved that smell, and now she took a deep breath, smiling as she looked around at the displays of blooms. The gerberas were wilting.

Annie took them out of the window, removing some of the deadheads and putting some plant feed in the vase. She had several bouquets to make up that morning, and humming to herself, she made her way into the storeroom behind the counter, where rolls of colored tissue paper, cellophane, and twine stood waiting. She was just deciding which bouquet to make up first when the sound of the bell above the store door signaled the arrival of her first customer.

"I'll be with you in a moment. Please, do just browse," she called out.

To her surprise, the bell above the door jangled again, suggesting the customer had left as quickly as they had entered. Annie shook her head, putting down the vase of gerberas and stepping back out behind the counter.

There was no one there. She rolled her eyes, wondering why people were so impatient. But as she was about to return to the storeroom, a sound caused her to startle. It was the sound of a *boppli* crying – right there in the store.

"What on earth?" she exclaimed to herself, looking around her in confusion, wondering if someone was playing a joke on her.

But it was then that she saw it – a Moses basket, placed among the vases of flowers displayed in the window, and in it lay a *boppli*...

CHAPTER TWO

*A*nnie stared at the *boppli* in astonishment. It was tiny – perhaps only a week or two old – and it was feeling feisty, its cry grew louder, piercing the calm of the store. Annie rushed to the window display, removed the basket, and took the *boppli* into her arms.

"There, there, shush now. Where have you come from?" she whispered, cradling the *boppli*, and looking down at it in utter disbelief. Her heart was pounding and she felt a touch of panic but she forced it down.

She glanced out of the window for any sign of whoever had left the basket in the store. At the same time, she bounced the *boppli*, who was quietened now, and she placed him – or her, for she was unsure – back in the basket before hurrying to the door. She opened it to find Monica serving a customer at the stall.

"Are you all right?" Monica asked, as Annie looked back and forth, left and right across the market square.

"Did you just see someone come into the store? A woman with a basket?" Annie asked.

"I've been serving customers, Annie. I haven't seen anyone," Monica replied.

Annie liked Monica, but she could be a gossip, and instead of explaining the situation to her, she merely nodded and returned inside, just as the *boppli* began to cry again. She picked him up – for she had now decided he was a boy, given the blue knitted hat on his head – and shushed him.

"I wasn't expecting you to arrive this morning – you've come with the stork," she said, laughing at the thought of how surreal it was to find a *boppli* in a Moses basket amongst the chrysanthemums.

But this was no joke – this was a very real problem. Annie did not know what to do or who to go to for help. The *boppli* had been abandoned, and she had no idea of its parentage. She had never taken care of a *boppli* and knew nothing of what was required. The little one was now calm, resting quietly in her arms. His features were so small and perfect, and he had a dimple on his chin, blue eyes stared up at her with a look of wonder in them. Annie smiled, leaning down to kiss him.

"We'll find someone to help you," she whispered, just as the bell above the store door jangled.

Annie looked around in alarm, only to find Sarah Beiler standing before her. The bishop's *fraa* stared at her in astonishment.

"Annie... I didn't realize..." she began, even as Annie tried to make excuses.

"He's not mine," she exclaimed, laughing at the absurdity of the situation.

"But... are you looking after him for someone?" Sarah asked.

Annie shook her head. "*Nee*... he just appeared amongst the flowers. Someone left him... I just found him now," she said.

It was all too surreal, and yet it was very real, too. Annie was holding a *boppli* – a *boppli* abandoned by its *mamm*, and she did not know what to do about it.

Sarah Beiler hurried to her side, glancing down at the sleeping *boppli*, and looking up at Annie in astonishment.

"A foundling. How very strange. I don't know of anyone due to have a *boppli* in Faith's Creek at the moment, but to abandon it... the poor thing," she said, shaking her head in disbelief.

"But what do I do? What does anyone do when they find a *boppli* abandoned in their store?" Annie asked, fighting down her panic.

The enormity of the situation was now sinking in. She was holding a boppli – a living, breathing, needing, *boppli*. She knew nothing about being a *mamm*, let alone what was required for a newborn *kinner*.

"It's all right, you're not alone." Sarah reached out and touched her arm, offering support. "I'm not going to just leave you here with it. We shouldn't call it "it" – a boy, by the look of it, though there's no indication of a name. For now, we'll call him Esau," Sarah said.

Annie nodded, for she knew the biblical reference. Esau was the unexpected child of Rebekah, the brother of Jacob – and this *boppli* was certainly unexpected.

"He'll need feeding, and he can't just stay in the basket all day. I've got bouquets to make up," Annie said, glancing around the store and thinking of the dozen different jobs she was meant to be doing. Though she knew the *boppli* needed caring for, she couldn't just abandon her customers.

Sarah was looking at her and there was something about her calm and easy manner that made Annie relax. The bishop's *fraa* would take care of this. She would take Esau and soon, this would just be an exciting morning and she could get back to her life.

"I've got some things over at the house," Sarah said. "We keep them for new *mamms* who might be struggling to make ends meet with another mouth to feed. I'll make up a bottle with some warm milk and bring a few things over. He seems happy at the moment. Put him back in the basket and wait for me to come back. I'll ask Bishop Beiler if he knows of any expectant *mamms*. After all, we want to find the real *mamm*, if we can." With a last smile, Sarah hurried out of the store, Annie was left alone with Esau.

Panic clawed at her throat. That was not what she expected, she had thought that Sarah would take Esau with her. What was she to do?

CHAPTER THREE

*A*nnie closed her eyes and took three deep breaths. It was a technique her *mamm* had taught her. She had always said, that if you have a problem, one that was eating you up inside, you just had to breathe deeply and let it go to *Gott*.

Opening her eyes, she could see that Esau was asleep, and looked so peaceful, cradled in the basket. She sighed, she would get through this and from now on must think more of the *boppli* than herself. None of this was his fault. He was oblivious to everything going on around him. As long as he was fed and warm, Esau would be happy.

"But that doesn't mean I am, though," Annie said out loud. As soon as the words were out of her mouth, she was angry at herself. This was a selfish way to think and she must stop it. The Amish way was to serve and this little one needed help. It was her responsibility to give it — *until Sarah takes him away*, her mind added at the end.

Her thoughts turned to the *boppli's mamm* – why had she chosen the flower store as the place to leave him? It all seemed very strange, even as Annie felt terribly worried about the state of the woman's health. To give birth was no easy matter, and to recover alone was even harder. Somewhere out there, the woman was scared – hiding, perhaps even fleeing forever.

Realizing that her own problems were the least in this matter, Annie closed her eyes and began to pray to *Gott*. She had a devout and lively faith, and she prayed for the *mamm* and for Esau, asking *Gott* to watch over them both and to give her the strength and courage she needed for what lay ahead. It would have been the easiest thing in the world to summon the authorities and hand the *boppli* over. But Annie was not about to shrink from the responsibility given to her – she would follow her heart, just as her *mamm* had taught her to.

And right now, my heart's telling me that Esau needs someone to love him and take care of him, she thought to herself, opening her eyes just as Esau began to cry.

She returned to the basket, picking up the *boppli* and shushing him.

"I don't think I'm going to get many bouquets of flowers made this morning, am I?" she asked him, smiling down at the chubby little face. He was trying to smile but it was hard, he was obviously getting hungry and his face kept scrunching into a wail. Shushing him against her, she did her best to keep him happy.

It was not long before Sarah Beiler returned with a large bag under her arm. It contained two warm bottles of milk, a blanket – made by the quilting circle of whom Sarah had often spoken of to Annie during the conversations over the flowers – diapers, and a small teddy bear with a smiling face, which Sarah placed into the basket.

"There's plenty more I can bring, but we'll start with the basics first. Do you want to feed him, or shall I?" Sarah asked.

Annie had never fed a *boppli* before. She had rarely held one – save for the newborns of their neighbors back in Oregon, passed from arm to arm – but something told her she should be the one to give Esau his bottle. Taking it, she held it to his lips, praying he would take it.

"Oh... that's what he wanted," she exclaimed, as he began to suck hungrily from the bottle.

Sarah smiled. "I'm glad. Food, and warmth, that's what a *boppli* needs. Most other things are secondary, apart from love, of course," she said.

Annie nodded. She already felt a bond towards the *boppli* in her arms. He was so fragile, so innocent, so helpless, and she only wanted to do the right thing for him.

"I can show him love," Annie said, surprising herself as she looked at Sarah.

"You already are. I know this wasn't exactly what you were expecting when you opened the store this morning," Sarah said.

Annie laughed. "I wasn't expecting it at all, *nee*. But... we don't always get to choose what *Gott* has in store for us, do we?" she asked.

"You're right there, Annie. I asked Bishop Beiler if he knew of any women expecting, but he didn't. I'm not sure where *boppli* Esau came from, but he's here, and it seems *Gott* means for us to take care of him. At least for now. The bishop will talk to the authorities and see if any are missing. I'll keep asking around – we can't keep

19

him a secret. You can't hide a *boppli* for long," Sarah said.

Annie placed the now-sleeping Esau back in the basket with his teddy bear.

She could only imagine the reaction in Faith's Creek at the news of such a strange arrival in their midst. There would be gossip and conjecture but the *boppli* knew nothing of it, even as she wished he could talk and tell them where he came from.

"We'll do our best for him," she said, smiling down at Esau, and praying that *Gott* would bless him – and her – in all that was to come.

CHAPTER FOUR

"That's all the back shelves stacked now, Joseph. I'll go home for my meal if that's all right? I'll only be an hour or so," Marshall Lehman said, calling out to his fellow counter clerk in the mercantile store.

Joseph Peters looked up and nodded.

"Thank your *mamm* for those peanut butter squares she sent – they were delicious," he called out, waving to Marshall.

"You'll get plenty more of them with that kind compliment – she likes people who like her baking," Marshall replied.

"I *do* like her baking. My *mamm* burns everything she touches. She'd burn water for boiling an egg if my *daed* let her near the stove. See you later," Joseph called out.

Marshall chuckled and pulled his hat off the hook, and pushed it down over his thick black hair. He must get a haircut or his *mamm* would be after him. She loved cooking but she was no pushover.

Stepping out, he took in a big breath and looked up to feel the sun on his face. It was a bright, sunny spring day in Faith's Creek and the market square was busy. Marshall had worked at the mercantile store since leaving school, and he knew most of the community. He waved to Monica Hertz at her wool stall as he passed.

"Tell your *mamm* I've got the green yarn she wanted," she called out.

"*Denke*, I will – she's talked about nothing else but the jumper she's going to make me. I hope it's not *too* green," he called back.

Monica smiled. "I'm sure you'll look very fetching in it," she called back.

Marshall shook his head and smiled. He knew better than to pick the wool up and deny his *mamm* the visit to the store.

His stomach was rumbling, and his thoughts were turning to the midday meal. His *mamm* had promised him roast chicken and dumplings, and Marshall had been looking forward to it all morning. As he crossed the market square, he glanced in the direction of the new flower store which had opened on the opposite side to the mercantile. It was run by a pretty, petite woman with a determined smile. Once he had seen a lock of deep red hair, it reminded him of autumn leaves and suited her so much with her pale skin and red lips. What was wrong with him? Thinking such thoughts about the newcomer, Annie Lapp!

She had moved to Faith's Creek from Oregon three months previously. That was as much as Marshall knew about her – though he would dearly have liked to know more. She had always been pleasant towards him, but Marshall was far too shy to approach her and strike up a conversation.

Just like with every woman you've ever liked, he thought to himself, sighing at his inability to talk to women.

It was silly, but he was painfully shy, and at the age of twenty-four, he was yet to have experienced any form of meaningful relationship. It was not through lack of suitors – his *mamm* had seen to it he was introduced to any number of young women. She told him that he was handsome and strong with a smile that lit up his face, but she was his *mamm*, after all!

He had sat through many an evening social in one of the barns with the express intention of meeting a suitable companion. But so far, all his attempts had come to nothing, and Marshall was beginning to wonder if there was something wrong with him.

"You just haven't found the right one yet. Be bold, make mistakes," his *mamm* had told him, but Marshall was too afraid of being hurt to do so.

The flower store owner was a case in point. Marshall desperately wanted to talk to her, but he could simply not find the right words to do so. In his bolder moments, he had thought of asking her on a picnic by the creek or to accompany him to one of the board games nights run by Bishop Beiler and his *fraa*, but his confidence always failed him. Now, Marshall felt certain he would never speak to Annie in words of more than two syllables. But as he crossed the market square that afternoon, he caught sight of Annie, and what he saw made him stare in astonishment – she was carrying a *boppli* in a basket, accompanied by Sarah Beiler.

"I didn't know she was married," he said to himself. His heart sank as he realized what this meant.

On the bright side, he had been saved from making an utter fool of himself. If Annie had a *boppli*, she was married, and that meant she would not be going on a picnic with him by the creek or playing board games with him in one of the barns. In many ways, the sight was a relief – as well as a disappointment. His *mamm* could no longer put pressure on him, for he had made the mistake of telling her of his burgeoning feelings for the flower store owner.

"Just speak to her," his *mamm* had said, but it was never going to be as easy as that.

Marshall watched as the two women hurried across the market square and disappeared in the direction of the cottage Marshall knew Annie had rented from Ezekiel Bride. He sighed and shook his head – whoever her husband was, he was a lucky man.

"And I've saved myself from an embarrassment," Marshall told himself, as he turned in the opposite direction towards home.

He and his *mamm* shared a house on the edge of Faith's Creek, with views across the rolling landscape of cornfields and meadows. Marshall had grown up there, and whilst he had lost his *daed* at an early age, his *kinnerhood* had been a happy one. He had no brothers or sisters, just him and his *mamm,* and together, they had always been happy.

The house was surrounded by a large garden, where Marshall grew vegetables, and he paused, stooping to inspect his cabbages, smiling to himself at the sight of how big they were growing.

"That's a prize at the vegetable show," he said out loud. Even though they were only seedlings at the moment, he could hope.

He made his way up the steps onto the porch, pulling off his boots. The smell of cooking wafted from the house, and he opened the door, calling to his *mamm* as he went.

"I'm home, *Mamm.* I haven't got long, though. Oh, Joseph says to tell you how much he enjoyed those peanut butter squares. I told him to be careful – you'd only send more for his compliments. I think he was hoping for it," Marshall called out, padding across the parlor in his socks and into the kitchen.

But as he entered the kitchen, he was surprised to find his *mamm* was not alone but joined by his cousin, Eve.

The sight of her was a shock, her normally ruddy face was pale, her long black hair was tied back behind her, and she had put on weight but was wearing a large *Englischer* dress that hid her figure. There were blue smudges under her eyes and a sickly look to her skin.

Marshall had not seen Eve for several years. She had been living in Philadelphia after the death of her parents, and the last Marshall had heard of her, she had been working as a waitress in a restaurant. His aunt and uncle had left Faith's Creek – and their faith – behind when Eve was only a *kinner*. He was surprised to find her sitting in the kitchen eating the roast chicken and dumplings meant for his noontime meal. A wave of shame washed over him, she looked terrible, and it seemed she had been crying.

"Look who's come to stay," his *mamm* said, looking up at Marshall with an anxious expression on her face.

His *mamm* was a practical sort of woman, not usually given over to emotion, but she looked worried now, her hand on Eve's shoulder, comforting her as she ate.

"Eve? We weren't expecting you, were we?" Marshall asked, wondering if he had forgotten the news of his cousin's arrival.

"No... you weren't... it's awfully kind of you... well, of Aunt Linda. Things haven't been going very well for me back in Philadelphia. I... I didn't have anywhere else to go. I've got no money – I lost my job," she said, as fresh tears rolled down her cheeks.

Marshall felt sorry for her. She had not had an easy life, he knew that, but it was still a surprise to see her sitting before him after having heard nothing from her in years.

"I'm sorry to hear that, Eve. I'm sure we'll do what we can to help you. We've got room, haven't we, *Mamm*?" he said.

His *mamm* nodded. "I've told Eve she can stay here as long as she needs to. We'll help her," Linda said.

Marshall slumped down in the chair opposite his cousin.

She was a pretty creature, though as far as Marshall knew, she had never had a suitor. But things were different in the world beyond the community of Faith's Creek. Marshall had spent his *rumspringa* in Detroit, working in an ice cream parlor, but had been only too glad to return home to the life he had always known. Some relished leaving behind the traditions of their fore-bears, even if for a short time, but Marshall had felt out of place and that those traditions were important, and it was by those traditions he lived.

"You don't look well, Eve," he said, for his cousin was very pale, and her hands were trembling.

"I think we might send for Doctor Yoder. He could take a look at you, Eve," Linda said.

At the mention of the doctor, Eve shook her head, a look of fear coming over her face.

"No... I don't need a doctor. I just want to rest after the journey. I'll go up to bed if that's all right?" she said, rising hurriedly to her feet.

"Of course, that's all right, Eve. You go up to bed if you want – I keep the guest room made up. I'll bring you some cocoa," Linda said.

Eve hurried off up the stairs, leaving the half-finished plate of roast chicken and dumplings behind.

Marshall looked anxiously at his *mamm*, who shook her head. "It's all a bit sudden, isn't it?" he asked.

There was worry in his *mamm's* eyes, but she nodded. "I don't know what to make of it. I was just going to make some more peanut butter squares when she appeared at the door. I was as surprised as you to see her. She didn't write. I've heard nothing from her in years, and now she turns up out of the blue. We'll take care of her, of course, but I don't know what's best for her in the long term. She can't stay here forever," she said.

Marshall ate his meal ponderously. The arrival of his cousin was the last thing he had been expecting that day, and whilst he wanted to help Eve, he was uncertain what he and his *mamm* could hope to do for her – apart from offering a bed and somewhere safe to stay.

"I'd better get back to work," Marshall said, glancing at the clock on the mantelpiece in the parlor, but as he returned to work that afternoon, all he could think about was the strange circumstances of his cousin's arrival... what had happened to her?

CHAPTER FIVE

"*O*h, Esau. I'm not sure what you want. Are you hungry? Are you cold? Or are you just making a fuss?" Annie asked, as she lifted the *boppli* from his crib and held him in her arms.

It had been three days since Annie had discovered Esau amongst the vases in the flower store window, but the mystery of where he came from, and why Annie should have found herself his guardian, remained. Bishop Beiler and Sarah had been amazing, finding and bringing over the crib and other bits that she would need. Sarah had even sat with her and helped her to change diapers and feed the *boppli*.

Doctor Yoder had checked him over and said that he was healthy and a lucky little boy. As the days passed Annie found herself getting more and more attached to him.

It was early morning, and Annie had been up most of the night with the *boppli*, who simply would not stop crying. She had fed him, wrapped him in two blankets, unwrapped him, held him, put him down, and fed him again – but nothing would stop his crying. Just then, a knock came at the door, and Annie went to answer it, holding the screaming *boppli* in her arms. Three women stood on the porch step, each holding a large box, and with smiles on their faces.

"*Gut* morning, Annie. We thought you might like some help," one of them – an elderly lady with dark hair beneath her *kapp* and a kindly face – said.

Annie looked at them in surprise, even as Esau began to cry.

"I..." she began, but another of the women – a tall woman with gray eyebrows over her blue eyes – interrupted.

"We should introduce ourselves – I'm Susanna Bontrager, this is Anna Troyer, and this is Lavinia Esch. We're from the quilting circle," she said, speaking in a tone such that it seemed Annie was supposed to be expecting them.

"Oh... the quilting circle?" Annie replied, trying to shush Esau, as the three women took a step forward with their boxes.

"Sarah asked us to call — we all know what it's like to have a newborn in the house. We're here to help," Susanna replied.

Annie stepped back — she could do nothing but invite them in, even as she had not asked for anyone's help with Esau. She was managing well enough on her own, at least she thought so, and whilst the *boppli* would not stop crying that morning, she did not believe she was doing anything wrong in terms of taking care of him.

"Well... that's really too kind of you," Annie said, as the three women filed into the cottage and placed the boxes down on the table.

They appeared to contain all manner of paraphernalia for the care of a newborn *boppli*, and now the three women rolled up their sleeves as though ready to set to work.

"Now, Annie, don't you worry about anything. We'll take care of Esau whilst you're at the flower shop. We can bath him, dress him, put him down to sleep, feed him – we'll do everything," the one called Anna said, and the other two nodded.

"And we'll give the cottage a *gut* clean, too. It looks like you've been far too busy to see to it," Lavinia said.

Annie was somewhat taken aback by this remark. The cottage was as it always was, albeit a little untidier. But it seemed the three women would not take *nee* for an answer, as they began fussing around, talking to one another as though Annie was not standing right in front of them.

"You see to the kitchen, Anna – we can always go out for supplies. I was thinking we could make a casserole. It's always *gut* to have a casserole when a newborn comes along, don't you think? I'll dust the parlor, shake out the rug, sweep out the stove. And why don't you see to the clothes, Susanna – we should've folded them all before we came. People have been so kind with their donations, but they all need sorting out," Lavinia said.

Annie was still holding Esau in her arms. She had not realized she was to be the subject of charity, nor that Esau's arrival was now common knowledge. Annie was used to managing on her own. She had come to Faith's Creek in the spirit of independence and did not wish to find herself at the center of everyone's attention – or charity.

"It's very kind of you, but I'm sure I can manage," she said, even as the three women set about their self-assigned tasks.

"It's not a case of managing, Annie. This *boppli's* part of our community. He's a gift from *Gott*, and we've all got to pull together and see he gets the best start possible. We all felt so sorry for you when we heard what had happened – finding a *boppli* abandoned in your store... it must've been terrible," Susanna said, shaking her head.

Annie realized she was not going to win against the charity. The women were very kind, and she knew Sarah Beiler had only been trying to help by enlisting the work of others in taking care of Esau. But casseroles, dusting, and charitable donations would not answer the burning question – where had Esau come from? It had been three days now, and still, there was no sign of an answer. Sarah Beiler had made inquiries, but there had been no reports of any pregnant women in Faith's Creek who might be struggling. Annie thought about Esau's *mamm* a great deal. To abandon your own *boppli* was a desperate cry for help, and she felt certain the woman had suffered a terrible tragedy.

"I'm managing. Esau's no trouble. He just cries a lot. But it's the *mamm* I feel sorry for. I just wish I'd seen her – spoken to her. Perhaps I could've helped her," Annie replied.

"She's probably halfway to Florida now. She won't care about the *boppli*. It's terrible to say it, but it's true," Anna said, shaking her head.

Annie was not convinced this was true. It was easy to judge a situation such as this – a *boppli* born in secret, perhaps out of wedlock, or in an abusive relationship. She had heard such stories existed and it made her shudder. Then it could be a widow, a *mamm* who simply could not cope with the thought of another mouth to feed. The arrival of a *boppli* did not always bring with it the joy it should, and the more she thought about Esau's *mamm*, the more she wanted to do something to help her.

"You go and open the flower store – the bouquet Sarah gave me for my birthday was beautiful, Annie. You've got such a talent, you really have. I'd hate to think your business suffered because of this. We'll take care of Esau for you today," Susanna said, holding out her arms for the *boppli*.

Annie felt reluctant to let Esau go. She had developed a bond with him, and it was not one she wished to give up so easily. He was her responsibility, and Annie was determined to manage on her own.

"I think I'll take him with me. He'll be quite all right. I can take a bottle with me, and he can sleep in his basket. I'm sure he'll settle down," she said, for Esau was still crying, even as she spoke.

Susanna raised her eyebrows, and the three women looked at one another.

"It's not easy bringing up a *boppli*, Annie. You're going to need a lot of help. There's no *daed* to help, and..." Lavinia began, but Annie was growing somewhat impatient.

"Not every *kinner* has a *daed*. I've got the flower store, and I manage perfectly well on my own. I don't need a man about the place... if that's what you mean," she replied.

"Lavinia didn't mean it like that, Annie. We just want to help, that's all," Susanna replied.

Annie sighed. She knew she would not convince them of her suitability alone. Women were to be pitied if they were forced to bring up a *kinner* alone, they wondered what she would do if Esau's *mamm* could not be found.

"And it's very kind of you, but I'm managing. I really am," Annie replied.

"Well... won't you at least let us make some meals for you and tidy the cottage? We've got all these things here, too – gifts from the women in the quilting circle. They all want to help," Susanna said.

Annie felt sorry for her attitude. It seemed she was tired and snappy and she smiled. "I'm sorry, I guess I'm a little irritable today. That *would* be very kind," Annie admitted, for she had not had time to cook a decent meal since Esau's arrival, and the cottage *was* somewhat untidy.

The three women smiled at her.

"All right, you take Esau to work, and we'll get started here," Anna said, and with a compromise reached, Annie placed Esau in the basket and put on her shawl, checking her *kapp* in the mirror.

She knew she looked tired, and she rubbed her eyes, smiling at her reflection. *I certainly never imagined this when I arrived in Faith's Creek,* she thought to herself.

Leaving the three women to their self-assigned tasks, Annie took the basket and stepped out onto the porch. It was another bright spring day in Faith's Creek, and the sun was shining down. As Annie made her way across the market square, she knew she was being looked at – Esau's arrival was common knowledge, and speculation as to his *mamm's* identity was rife.

"*Gut* morning, Annie. How are you getting on with the new arrival?" Monica asked as Annie unlocked the door of the flower store.

"Oh, I'm managing, I think. It's a steep learning curve, though. I didn't know anything about *bopplis* until a few days ago," Annie said.

Monica laughed. "When I had my first, it was like swimming in the dark. No one really prepares you for what it's like. Not really. You can read all the books you want, and take all the advice that's given. But it's not until you actually hold the little bundle in your arms that it becomes real," Monica said.

Annie nodded. She had known nothing about *bopplis*, and now Esau was her responsibility – he depended on her, and she knew it was up to her to take care of him until his real *mamm* could be found. Perhaps that was why she had been so reluctant to give up that responsibility to the women from the quilting circle. Annie had always been a determined sort, and now she thanked Monica for her words and took Esau into the flower store.

The scent of the blooms hung heavily in the air, and she placed the basket next to a vase of tulips, the petals of which were colored red and yellow.

"Well, then, it looks like you're here with me for the day. Are you going to sleep, or are you going to keep on making all that noise?" Annie asked, smiling down at Esau, who was gazing up at the flowers in the vase.

He seemed entranced by the colors. Annie moved several other vases to surround the basket with color. Esau stopped crying, his attention wholly taken by the colors all around him. Thankful for small mercies, Annie stepped away, quietly beginning her work at the counter, and occasionally glancing up to check on the *boppli*, who was now asleep.

I just hope I can do the right thing by him, she thought to herself, knowing Esau depended on her – and so did his *mamm*.

CHAPTER SIX

"*E*ve hasn't got out of bed all morning. I took her some coffee," Linda said to Marshal when he came home for lunch. "I just don't know what to do. She seems so sad, but she won't talk about it. It's like she's withdrawn into herself."

Marshall watched his *mamm* sigh and shake her head, but he also didn't know what to do.

It had been three days since Eve had come to stay with Marshall and his *mamm*, and she was yet to leave the house. She spent her days in bed, and Marshall had heard her crying at night. All she would say is that things went wrong for her in Philadelphia – she had lost her job and had nowhere else to go. The facts were sad in themselves, but they did not explain why Eve should withdraw into herself so much – she could find another job, and she could make a fresh start. There were plenty of jobs in Faith's Creek, and Marshall and his *mamm* had both told Eve they would help her. But nothing they said or did, seemed to alleviate her sorrow. Marshall could only wonder how long it would last. It was as though she was hiding something – a terrible secret she could not bear to share with anyone.

"And she still won't see Doctor Yoder?" Marshall asked, sitting down at the table as his *mamm* placed a plate of buttered noodles in front of him.

"If I suggest it, she looks horrified. *Nee*, she won't see the doctor, and she won't tell me what's wrong. I just wish... well, perhaps I should've been better at keeping in touch with her. I didn't know anything was going on. I thought she was happy in Philadelphia. But clearly, she wasn't," Linda replied, sighing, and sitting down opposite him.

"Don't blame yourself. There's nothing you could've done. They went off to Philadelphia. It was Aunt Pauline and Uncle Ronald who chose that life for her. It's often the way – people reject the faith, but they lose so much more than that. They lose community. I'm not surprised she was struggling after they died. She didn't have anyone, and it's a long way to Philadelphia from here," Marshall said, shaking his head.

His *mamm* sighed again, glancing towards the stairs leading up to the bedrooms.

"I'll take her some buttered noodles in a few minutes... anyway, how did work go today? Is Joseph still hankering after some peanut butter squares? I've not had time to do any baking since Eve arrived – my mind's been too distracted," she said.

"He's not stopped talking about them – but he did when he heard the news," Marshall said.

His *mamm* looked at him in surprise. "What news?" she asked.

"About the *boppli* they found in the flower store – you know the one I mean, it's only just opened a few months ago. Annie Lapp – she came from Oregon, I think. She found a *boppli* left in the store. No one knows whose it is," Marshall replied.

He had been surprised – and somewhat relieved – to hear the story from Monica Hertz that morning. She had told him Annie and Sarah Beiler were taking care of the foundling, and that the *mamm* had not yet been found.

43

"That's astonishing. I can't imagine what would make a woman do that," Linda exclaimed, shaking her head.

"She must've been desperate, I suppose. Perhaps she couldn't look after it. I feel sorry for her – and the *boppli*. It's so sad," Marshall said, for he had been thinking about the situation a great deal since Monica had told him the story.

"You're right – we shouldn't judge her. I'm glad the *boppli's* being taken *gut* care of, though. I'm sure they'll find the *mamm* in due course. You know Bishop Beiler, he won't rest if someone needs help. Anyway, she can't have just disappeared."

"*Nee*, she must be around somewhere, but who do we know who hasn't been to service for a while? It makes no sense." Marshal shook his head and then began his plate of noodles.

"I'd better take Eve something to eat. She can't just lie in bed all day. It's not *gut* for her," Linda said, rising to her feet and going to the stove, where the pan of buttered noodles stood, keeping warm on a low flame.

Marshall pondered to himself. He wanted to cheer his cousin up, and now he had an idea.

"I'll buy her some flowers. Didn't Aunt Pauline used to keep a garden?" Marshall asked, for he had a vague recollection of his *mamm* telling him about his aunt's prizewinning flowers.

"Oh, Pauline always loved her garden," she replied.

The two sisters had barely spoken since Marshall's aunt and uncle had rejected the faith. It was a source of pain for Marshall's *mamm*, even as she always said she prayed for Pauline every day.

"I'll buy her some flowers this afternoon from the flower store," he said.

Linda smiled. "That's very thoughtful of you, Marshall. I'm sure she'll appreciate it."

Marshall finished his meal, and bidding his *mamm* goodbye, he set off back in the direction of the market square. He did not know why he felt so nervous at the prospect of buying flowers. But the idea of speaking with Annie made him so. Previously, he had found no reason to do so – though he had tried. Buying flowers for Eve gave him an excuse to enter the flower store and speak with Annie directly.

Marshall knew it would be a perfunctory conversation – he would ask Annie for some flowers, she would give them to him, he would pay her and leave – but at least it would be an opportunity for her to realize he existed, and perhaps from there...

Oh... who am I kidding? Dozens of men go into that flower store every day to buy flowers. She won't give you a second thought, he told himself, shaking his head as he approached the flower store.

CHAPTER SEVEN

"*B*uying some flowers for your *mamm*?" Monica asked as Marshall hovered outside the store, feeling nervous.

"*Nee*... I... they're for my cousin, actually. She's come to stay with us and she's not feeling well," Marshall replied.

"That's kind of you, Marshall. You've always been thoughtful like that," Monica said, smiling at him.

"*Denke*." Taking a deep breath, Marshall opened the flower store door. A bell jangled overhead, and the cries of a *boppli* filled the air.

"Oh... and I just got him off to sleep," a voice from behind the counter exclaimed. Annie hurried towards a display of vases, in the midst of which was a basket in which the now crying *boppli* was lying. Marshall blushed, feeling terribly embarrassed.

"Oh, I'm sorry," he said, as Annie lifted the *boppli* out and shushed him.

She looked up at him and rolled her eyes. "It's all right. If it wasn't the bell, it would've been something else. I only need to breathe, and it wakes him up," she said, smiling at Marshall, who was feeling thoroughly foolish.

"Still... I didn't realize... I don't know much about *kinner*, and certainly not about *bopplis*," Marshall replied.

"You and me both – but I'm stuck with one. Now, what can I do for you?" Annie asked giving him such a smile that he felt weak at the knees.

Now she was looking at him and waiting for him to speak. All he could think was that she was so beautiful and if Marshall knew nothing about *bopplis*, he knew little about flowers, either. Marshall grew vegetables. He knew about those, but as for flowers, they were like a foreign country to him.

"I'd like some flowers," he said.

Annie laughed. "Why else would you come to a flower store?" she asked with a smile.

Marshall blushed. "I... they're for my cousin. She loves flowers... maybe some red ones," Marshall said, glancing at what he thought were bunches of tulips in a vase next to where the basket lay.

"Tulips? I could put some roses in there, too?" Annie replied.

Marshall nodded. It sounded like a nice idea, and he was happy for Annie to make up the bouquet as she suggested.

"That sounds lovely," he said.

The *boppli* was still crying, and to Marshall's surprise, Annie handed the bundle to him, before turning her attention to the bouquet.

"All right, let's see now – mainly tulips, and just a few roses, a little gypsophila, too, I think," she said, taking blooms from the different vases, and holding them up together in a bouquet.

Marshall looked down at the *boppli*. His eyes were open, and he was blowing bubbles. He had a dimple in his chin, a dimple that looked just like that of his cousin.

"He's a beautiful *boppli*," Marshall said.

To him, all *bopplis* looked the same. But he wanted to keep the conversation going, and a compliment seemed the best way.

Annie looked at him and smiled. "They all look the same to me," she said.

Marshall felt his cheeks heat. "You're right..." he replied, backtracking a little, as Annie wrapped the flowers in cellophane and tissue paper.

The bouquet looked beautiful, and Marshall felt certain it would bring a smile to his cousin's face.

"There we are. That's $15," Annie said.

Marshall handed over the money, still with the now quiet *boppli* cradled in his arm.

"You're quite the natural at that. Come back anytime you like," Annie said.

Marshall smiled. "I'd like that," he replied, and she smiled back at him.

He stood for a moment, wishing he knew better what to say or had the courage to be bold and ask her the question on the tip of his tongue.

"Is there anything else?" she asked.

Flustered, he shook his head. "*Nee*... but... *denke*, my cousin's going to love these," he said, handing Annie the *boppli*.

"I hope she feels better soon," Annie said.

Taking the bouquet of flowers, Marshall left the store.

Had he been bolder, he might have asked Annie to go on a picnic with him, or to one of Bishop Beiler's social evenings. But for now, Marshall was simply glad to have introduced himself.

"*She knows I exist,*" he told himself, as he made his way across the market square to the mercantile store.

"Are those for me?" Joseph asked as Marshall placed the bouquet behind the counter.

He laughed and shook his head. "*Nee*... but I'm glad I bought them," Marshall replied, hoping it would not be long before he found another reason to return to the flower store...

CHAPTER EIGHT

"*W*ell, wasn't he a nice young man?" Annie said as she placed Esau back in his basket.

The boppli looked up at her and blew bubbles, gurgling as she tickled him under the chin. Annie was glad the store clerk had called in that afternoon, even as she smiled at the thought of how nervous he had appeared. But the act of buying flowers for his cousin was a thoughtful one, and Annie could not help but admire him for that. She had noticed him several times, and now she stepped out of the flower store for a moment, catching Monica's eye as she was serving a customer.

"Did I just see Marshall Lehman coming out with a bunch of tulips?" Monica asked.

"You did – do you know him?" Annie asked because she was curious to learn more about the man she had just served.

"He's a *gut*, dependable sort. He lives with his *mamm*, Linda. His *daed* died when he was young. He's worked at the mercantile since he left school. I've always liked him. He's the sort to do anything for anyone. He grows vegetables and donates a lot of the surplus to the soup kitchen in Bird-in-Hand. But I didn't know he had a sweetheart," Monica replied.

"A sweetheart?" Annie asked, raising her eyebrows.

"Men buy flowers for their *mamms* and their sweethearts. Which one was it?" Monica asked.

Annie laughed. "Neither. It's for his cousin. He said she wasn't very well," Annie replied.

Monica looked at her in surprise.

"Oh... that's strange. I'm surprised she's here," she said.

Annie looked at her curiously. "Why's that? It doesn't seem strange to me," she replied.

Monica shook her head. "Marshall's *mamm* had a sister – Pauline, I think. She married an *Englischer* named Ronald Bermont. He set her mind against the faith, and the two of them left Faith's Creek when Eve – that's Marshall's cousin – was only a *boppli*. I don't think they've been back since – though they're dead now. I felt sorry for the *kinner* at the time. It's not right to be taken away from your community like that. I always wondered if she'd come back, but she never did... until now. But that's just like Marshall to think like that – how kind," Monica said, turning to serve a customer at the stall.

Annie had further questions for her, but the sound of Esau crying brought her attention back to the present, and calling out *denke* to Monica, she returned inside.

It turned out Esau was hungry, and Annie warmed a bottle for him, sitting in the storeroom on an upturned packing crate to feed him.

"There, now, that's better, isn't it?" she said, smiling down at him as he fed.

There were still bouquets to make up, but Annie's mind was elsewhere – she was thinking of Marshall – and with the bottle finished, she wrapped Esau in a sling so she could carry him as she worked. It was after three o'clock, and since Esau's arrival, Annie had missed her daily walk down to the creek and through the woods. She loved the rural setting of Faith's Creek – it was one of the reasons she had moved there – and with Esau asleep in the sling, Annie closed up the store and set off for a walk.

"You're closing early," Monica said, as Annie turned the key in the door.

"With everything that's been going on, I just feel like a walk," Annie replied.

Monica smiled at her. "You do right, Annie. I'll see you tomorrow," she said.

Bidding the stallholder *gutbye*, Annie made her way across the market square in the direction of the creek, carrying the sleeping Esau in the sling over her shoulder.

Several women stopped to thank her for what she was doing and assure her they were willing to help in any way necessary.

"You're doing *Gott's* work," one of them said, and several, men, too, stopped and looked at her, shaking their heads as though in solidarity with the prevailing opinion that the *boppli's mamm* was entirely to blame for the difficulties visited on Annie in this moment of need.

But Annie herself did not blame Esau's *mamm* – she felt sorry for her and would gladly have helped her in any way she could. But without any leads to go on, the mystery remained, and all Annie could do was take care of Esau as best she could – knowing she would never be short of advice should she require it. It was as though the whole community had adopted Esau as its own, and whilst Annie was grateful to them for their kindness, she was grateful for the peace afforded her by the creek. The sun was shining through the trees, casting dappled ripples on the water. Annie was humming to herself. It was a song her *mamm* used to sing to her as a *kinner*, a lullaby about a *boppli* floating in a basket down a stream.

"Do you like that, Esau?" she asked, as she felt the *boppli* stir in his sling.

Esau made a crying noise, and Annie feared she had woken him up, but he seemed to settle again, rocked by the motion as she walked along the path by the water's edge. Annie knew all the paths through the woods. She had explored them systematically since her arrival in Faith's Creek, taking one and then another, and finding circular walks of half an hour, an hour, or even two hours. One afternoon, Annie had walked so far, she had come to the outskirts of Bird-in-Hand, before catching a bus back to Faith's Creek. But this afternoon, Annie only wanted to stroll beneath the trees and enjoy being alone.

It's so beautiful down here. So peaceful, she thought to herself, as a fish jumped in the water, its silvery scales catching the sunlight.

But as it splashed back into the water, a sudden movement to Annie's left caused her to turn. To her surprise, she saw a young girl standing amongst the trees, watching her. Annie guessed she was around twenty years old. Her long black hair – not covered by a *kapp* – hung down over her shoulders, and she was wearing a baggy flowered dress that was not Amish. Annie had not seen her before, and she looked nothing like the women who frequented her flower store in the market square. But at the sight of Annie looking at her, the woman startled and turned to run.

"It's all right, I'm not going to hurt you," Annie called after her, but the woman was gone, and with a *boppli* on her back, Annie was not about to give chase.

How curious, she thought to herself, wondering who the woman could be.

She rarely met anyone walking by the creek, and now a sudden thought occurred to her – had the woman been following her? She had appeared distressed, upset even, and now Annie undid the sling from her back and took Esau in her arms.

"Do you think that was your *mamm*?" she asked.

Esau looked up at her, his eyes open, and blowing bubbles from his mouth. She smiled at him, cradling him in her arms, as she thought about the woman who had been watching her so intently.

Sarah Beiler and the others had been unable to discover anything as to Esau's *mamm's* identity, but Annie had been convinced she was someone local to Faith's Creek. If the investigations as to Esau's *mamm* had been confined to members of the Amish community, then it was no wonder they had not discovered the woman's identity. The woman who had followed her had the appearance of an *Englischer* – she was not Amish – and now Annie wondered if the *boppli's mamm* was perhaps a confused youngster from Bird-in-Hand who had panicked at the thought of giving birth and done the only thing she could think of, abandoning the *boppli* amongst the vases in the flower store.

Poor thing, she must be terrified, Annie thought to herself.

She walked on a little way by the water's edge, but her thoughts were distracted by the memory of the woman, and now she resolved to do what she could to find her.

I've got to. I can't just pretend as though Esau's my own son, she thought to herself.

Annie had been surprised at the force of the feelings which had overtaken her. She loved Esau as though he was her own, and she would have done anything for him, and for his *mamm*. He knew nothing of what had happened to him, and when he cried, it was not for affection from the one who had carried him for nine months long, but for the practical needs of everyday life.

As she returned to the cottage that afternoon – finding it spick and span, with a casserole sitting on the kitchen table waiting to be warmed through – Annie prayed for the woman she had seen by the creek, that her identity might be revealed, and that if she *was* Esau's *mamm*, that she would have the courage to admit it, and do the right thing by her son.

CHAPTER NINE

arshall was pleased with the bouquet of flowers – and the fact that he had finally summoned the courage to speak to Annie, albeit in a transactional manner. The roses had a sweet perfume to them, and Annie had wrapped the bouquet in pretty orange tissue paper. Marshall was certain they would bring a smile to Eve's face, but as he came to the garden gate, his *mamm* came hurrying to meet him.

"You haven't seen Eve, have you? I wondered if she'd come to the mercantile for some reason," she said.

Marshall shook his head. He had seen no sign of Eve on his way back from the market square, nor had she been to the mercantile.

"Isn't she here?" he asked, but his *mamm* shook her head.

"*Nee*, she left without telling me. I was in the kitchen cleaning, I went up to take her some coffee and she was gone. She's not herself. Though I'll admit, I don't really know what *herself* should be. She's... there's something wrong with her. I'm worried about her, though. She doesn't know Faith's Creek – what if she's got lost?"

Marshall could hear the fear in his *mamm's* voice, and he put his hand on her shoulder, trying to reassure her.

"She can't have gone far – probably just for a walk. I'll go and look for her, all right?" he said.

His *mamm* nodded. "That's very kind of you Marshall – and what beautiful flowers you've got there."

"Oh... they're for Eve. Will you put them in water for me? I met the new *boppli* – the one we were talking about, at the flower store," Marshall said.

His *mamm* smiled. Marshall knew she was hoping to be a *grossmammi* one day. She loved *kinner* and *bopplis* in particular.

"I just hope they find the *mamm*. The poor little thing must be so confused. Is she coping – the owner of the flower store, I mean?" Linda asked.

Marshall thought back to his encounter with Annie and smiled. She seemed to be a woman with strong determination and a will to succeed. The arrival of a *boppli* had not appeared to phase her, and she seemed to be taking it in her stride.

"I think she's coping very well, all things considered... anyway, I should go and look for Eve, and I was thinking... maybe I should go and speak to Bishop Beiler about Eve. She didn't ask to leave Faith's Creek. It's clear she's got no direction, and she's going through some kind of crisis. I wonder if coming back to the faith might help her," he said.

The thought had been on Marshall's mind since his cousin's unexpected return. He had always practiced his faith. It came naturally to him and was as much a part of everyday life as working at the mercantile store or digging vegetables in the garden. Faith was a gift he had always been grateful for, and he could not imagine his life without *Gott* at the center. He had always felt sorry for those who had come to reject their way of life. They were often bitter and resentful. Eve had not chosen to reject her faith – she had been given no choice – and Marshall wondered if now, in whatever crisis she was experiencing – the time had come to return to trust in *Gott*.

"I think that's a *gut* idea. I'll wait here, and we'll see if she comes back. You go and look for her, then speak to Bishop Beiler," she replied.

Marshall nodded, and turned back down the garden path, glancing at his vegetable patch as he went. He had neglected it since Eve's arrival, and weeds were starting to grow amongst the cabbages. He turned right out of the gate, intending to take a route along the path by the creek and back up to the market square. He had no idea where his cousin might have gone, and with her state of mind, as it was, he feared for her safety.

I just don't understand what's wrong with her. I suppose people have breakdowns, or just can't cope with life anymore. Without faith, there's just the wilderness, Marshall thought to himself.

As he walked, he prayed, asking *Gott* to bless Eve and bring her safely home. He walked along the path leading through the cornfields towards the creek, where the crop was already at knee height, swaying gently in the breeze. It was a warm day, and the sun felt pleasant on his face.

He met no one by the water's edge, as he made his way along the familiar path, looking this way and that for any sign of his cousin. But she was nowhere to be found, and by the time he came to the market square, Marshall was growing increasingly worried.

"You haven't seen a girl, about twenty years old, with long black hair, have you, Monica?" Marshall asked as he came to the stall selling yarn and knitting supplies.

"Your cousin?" Monica asked, and Marshall looked at her in surprise.

He did not remember mentioning his cousin to Monica, and he nodded.

"That's right... how did you know?" he asked, and Monica smiled and nodded toward the flower store.

"Annie mentioned you'd come to buy some flowers for her," she said.

Marshall smiled. "I... did," he said, surprised to think of Annie mentioning him at all, let alone remembering such a detail as who the bouquet was for.

"I haven't seen her, though. Annie said she wasn't well, though," Monica said.

"She's not, and she's gone off on her own. We don't know where she is," Marshall replied, looking around at the other stalls which stood on the market square.

But there was no sign of Eve anywhere. She was gone, and Marshall knew the best thing he could do was go and speak with Bishop Beiler. Amos would know what to do.

CHAPTER TEN

"*I*'ll keep an eye out for her," Monica promised.

Marshall thanked her before hurrying off in the direction of the bishop's house.

He did not wish to disturb Bishop Beiler. He was an important man, with much responsibility, but Marshall knew he would take his worries seriously, and as he hurried up the path to the bishop's house, the door was opened by Sarah, the bishop's *fraa*.

"Oh, Marshall – I was just coming to the mercantile store. I've broken so many plates recently, we've only got three left. It's high time I bought a new set. Is something troubling you?" she asked.

Marshall nodded. He did not want to be a burden, but he was so worried about Eve, and now the bishop, too, came to the door.

"*Gut* day, Marshall. What can we do for you?" he asked.

Marshall had always liked Bishop Amos Beiler. He was a kindhearted man, a true pastor, and a man of *Gott*.

"I'm sorry to bother you, Bishop Beiler – Mrs. Beiler. But it's my cousin, Eve. You might've heard, she's come to stay with us from Philadelphia. We weren't expecting her. She turned up out of the blue, and she was suffering something terrible. She won't hear of having Doctor Yoder come and examine her, but I wonder if it's more of a spiritual problem than a physical one. She's gone missing, though... well, she went out without telling my *mamm*, and we don't know where she's gone," Marshall said, the words tumbling out of him in a garbled mass.

Bishop Beiler and his *fraa* exchanged glances.

"Slow down, young man, you know us, it's Amos and Sarah."

"Sorry, Bi... Amos." Marshall felt his cheeks heating and he dropped his head, this was *nee* time for his shyness.

67

"I knew she'd come from Philadelphia, and I remember your Aunt Pauline well," Amos said. "It was such a tragedy. I don't begrudge anyone marrying the person they love, but your Uncle Ronald turned your aunt against the faith, and the community she'd always known. I felt so sorry for your *mamm*. You and Eve were just *kinner* when it happened. It was a real tragedy," Amos said, shaking his head which made his long white beard brush against his shirt.

Marshall nodded, seeing the kindness in the bishop's blue eyes. He knew how much his aunt's behavior had upset his *mamm*. There had been plenty of arguments over the years, and there had been no reconciliation before his Aunt Pauline had died. In helping Eve, Marshall knew his *mamm* was trying to make amends for that parting of ways, and Marshall was determined to do what he could to help.

"I just don't know what's wrong with Eve. She's been in a terrible state. She stays in bed the whole time, she's withdrawn and anxious. It's like something terrible happened to her, but she won't talk about it," Marshall said, feeling utterly helpless to know what to do to help his cousin.

"You can't force her to reveal whatever it is she's hiding. I know you're worried about her, but right now, you're doing the best thing for her," Amos said. "Come inside and sit."

"Yes, go through. I will make coffee and I have some cookies just out of the oven," Sarah said.

Marshall followed the bishop through to the big polished table; he did not understand what Amos meant. In his mind, he was doing nothing for Eve, because he did not know what to do to help her.

"But I'm not doing anything," he replied as he slumped down in a chair across from the bishop.

Amos gave him a sympathetic smile.

"You're loving her, aren't you? You and your *mamm* – you've given her a place to stay, you've taken care of her, you've prayed for her, you've been there for her in her hour of need. That's what counts, Marshall. I know it's frustrating when you don't know the "whys," but it's the "how" that matters when someone's suffering. Just being there for Eve. Loving her. Sometimes, that's all we can do. I know you're worried about her going missing – we'll keep an eye out, and we'll tell others to do so, too. Go home and wait for her – I think she'll probably turn up soon," Amos said.

Marshall nodded. He was still worried, but he was grateful to Bishop Beiler for his advice. Eve would speak about her problems when the time was right – what he and his *mamm* had to do was love her. That was what *Gott* was calling them to do, and Marshall was determined to fulfill that calling.

For a few minutes, they drank coffee, munched on the cookies, and talked about the district. Then, he thanked the bishop and his *fraa*, and made his way home, praying Eve would have returned, and as he made his way up the garden path, he saw her through the parlor window, sitting at the table.

A wave of relief came over him, and he hurried up the steps onto the porch, pulled off his boots, and went inside. Eve was drinking a cup of coffee, and Linda was fussing around her.

"Eve – we've been worried about you," Marshall exclaimed, as Eve looked up at him.

"Oh... I'm sorry. I just went for a walk. I didn't realize you'd worry," she said, glancing at Linda, who had obviously made her feelings on the matter clear already.

Marshall remembered Bishop Beiler's words and smiled at his cousin as he sat down opposite her.

"It's all right. But we care about you, Eve. We were worried something had happened to you," he said.

"I suppose I'm just used to doing what I feel like. I'm sorry if you were worried," Eve replied.

She appeared to have been crying, her eyes were red and her cheeks flushed. Marshall could only feel sorry for her, and the burden she bore – whatever it was.

"It's all right. You're back now, and oh... I've got something for you," Marshall exclaimed, remembering the flowers.

His *mamm* had put them in a vase of water in the kitchen, and now he brought them out, presenting them to his cousin, who received them with delight.

"Oh, Marshall... that's so kind of you. They're beautiful," she exclaimed, breathing in the scent, and smiling.

It was a genuine smile, a smile Marshall had not seen in the course of his cousin's stay with them, and he was glad to have done something to bring some cheer to her.

"I got them from the flower store on the market square. I'm glad you like them," he said.

At the mention of the flower store, his cousin looked up in surprise.

"Oh... yes, of course... the flower store. I wonder... could we go there together?" she asked.

Marshall was pleased – he had been trying to think of an excuse to return to the flower store and see Annie. If Eve wanted to go there, he would be only too happy to accompany her.

"Certainly – I'd be happy to take you. We just want to look after you, Eve," Marshall said.

She smiled once again.

"You've both been so kind. I'm sorry for running off like that. I really am very grateful," she said.

Marshall smiled back at her. "We'll go and buy some flowers together tomorrow," he replied, glad of an excuse to return to the flower store and see Annie again...

CHAPTER ELEVEN

"**B**ut if we can't find his *mamm*, what then?" Annie asked as she and Sarah Beiler sat drinking coffee in the storeroom of the flower store.

Esau was asleep in his basket. Sarah had brought a pile of clothes – all made by the quilting circle – to add to the many donations she had already received, and the two women had been sorting through them over the course of the morning. The talk had naturally turned to Esau's future.

It had been two weeks now since Annie had discovered him amongst the vases in the window of the flower store, and the mystery as to where the *boppli* had come from remained.

"I'd hoped we could resolve this quickly," Sarah said. "Amos spoke to the authorities, they think it must be an Amish *boppli*, which is a *gut* thing."

"A *gut* thing?" Annie asked because she had expected the authorities to care more about the *boppli*.

"It means that Esau can stay with us, otherwise, he would go into care and it might be *gut*... but it might not." Sarah sipped her coffee. "I thought we'd find Esau's *mamm* easily enough ourselves. It's a small community, and it shouldn't have been difficult. But if the *mamm* isn't Amish, we're going to have trouble finding her – especially if she's come from somewhere else with the express intention of leaving the *boppli*."

Annie, too, was now relieved the authorities would leave it to them. The thought of Esau being taken into care scared her. He would go to an orphanage or foster parents. He would be taken from the community, and grow up knowing nothing of the Amish way of life. The woman – whoever she was – who had left him in the flower store had chosen Faith's Creek as the place to leave her *boppli*. That had surely meant something, and Annie hoped it meant Esau's *mamm* had trusted the community of Faith's Creek to take care of him.

"I don't want him to go to an orphanage. I've grown attached to him. I couldn't imagine life without him," Annie replied, glancing into the basket at the sleeping *boppli*. His little feet had kicked off his quilt as he dreamed in his sleep. He was oblivious to everything going on around him, and for that, she was pleased.

Annie continued to be surprised by the force of her feelings towards Esau. When she held him in her arms, she felt an overwhelming sense of maternal care for him. She loved him as though he were her own, and as things stood, he was. He had no one else but her. He depended on her for everything, and Annie was not about to let him down.

"We don't want that either. Everyone's saying the same. He's a part of this community now, and we've been given the duty of taking care of him. *Nee*... he won't go to an orphanage. It hasn't come to that yet. We'll keep looking for his *mamm*," Sarah said, taking up another basket of *boppli* clothes to sort and fold.

But another thought occurred to Annie, one which could have the same consequences as not finding Esau's *mamm* – if she was found, what if she did not want anything to do with the *boppli* she had left in the flower store... or what if she wanted to take him far away?

75

"If we do find Esau's *mamm*, what happens then?" Annie asked.

Either way, she would be forced to give up the *boppli*. She could not keep him, could she?

To find his *mamm* risked either rejection on her part, leading to some childless couple from the district taking Esau, or a reconciliation in which Esau was returned to her. Annie had not expected to feel like this. She had taken on the responsibility for Esau in a purely practical manner, never imagining her feelings for him would grow so strong.

"Well... I suppose we would need to help her understand what's happened. She might regret leaving Esau here, or... she might want nothing to do with him. Either way, she needs to understand what she's done, and the consequences of that," Sarah replied.

Annie sighed, glancing again at the sleeping *boppli*, and wishing life could be as simple as she had dreamed it to be. Leaving Oregon had meant a new start for Annie. She had put the past behind her and was determined to build a new life for herself – a life of independence. But the arrival of Esau had changed that, and despite her best attempts at maintaining a practical demeanor, Annie's feelings had overtaken her.

"It's just... well, I can't help but feel something for him. I... I love him," she admitted.

Sarah smiled. "I know you do – you've shown it in everything you've done for him. You couldn't have done more, Annie. How couldn't you love him? And as far as he's concerned, you're his *mamm*. You're the one who comes to him when he cries, who holds him and makes him feel safe. It's you that feeds him, bathes him, and kisses him *gutnight*. Giving birth isn't just what makes you a *mamm*, Annie – it's love, too," Sarah said, and she placed her hand on Annie's and smiled.

Annie felt tears welling up in her eyes. It was true – she loved Esau as though he were her own. He *was* her own, and she would have done anything for him.

"I do love him, and I'd do anything for him," she replied.

"I know you would."

They finished folding the clothes. Annie still had lots of work to do in the flower store, and Sarah bid her *gutbye*, promising to call into the store the following day.

"It's very kind of you," Annie said, as she bid Sarah goodbye.

"And what you're doing is kind, too, Annie. I know it's hard work, but it's *Gott's* work, and you're blessing Esau with it. I'm sure I won't be the only one calling in – at this rate, we'll be able to open our own *boppli* wear store," Sarah said, laughing and shaking her head.

Annie saw her to the door, watching her leave, as she thought of the dozen different jobs she had to do. There were bouquets to make up for several anniversaries and wreaths to make for an *Englischer* couple who were going to visit their family graves. The flowers in the vases all needed seeing, and new stock was due to arrive at any moment.

How would she cope?

"One thing at a time," she told herself, just as Esau began to cry.

CHAPTER TWELVE

*A*nnie took a deep breath, remembering Sarah's words. Taking care of the *boppli* was a responsibility given to her by *Gott*. It was her duty – and joy. Annie made her way into the storeroom, smiling down at Esau, who was now happily awake and blowing bubbles.

"Did you just want to say "hello" to me? Reminding me you're here, were you?" she said, picking him up and bouncing him in her arms.

He made another gurgling noise – a sign he was happy, she had come to realize – and she was about to lay him down when the jangle of the bell above the door announced the arrival of a customer. Knowing Esau would inevitably begin to cry if she laid him down in the basket, Annie carried him out into the store, where, to her immense surprise, she saw Marshall, accompanied by the woman who had followed her by the creek.

The woman was staring at her, but Marshall seemed oblivious to their connection, smiling as Annie tried to maintain her composure.

"Hello, again... we wanted some more flowers. This is my cousin, Eve – the one I mentioned," Marshall said.

Annie had a feeling of foreboding, that she pushed down and she managed a smile. "It's... nice to meet you. I'm sorry to hear you weren't feeling well. Are you feeling better now?" she asked.

Eve nodded. "A little better, thank you," she said, her eyes fixed on Esau.

"I was thinking white flowers would be nice today. Something for my *mamm*. Lilies, perhaps. She loves fragrance," Marshall said, gazing around at the vases of flowers.

Annie was distracted by her thoughts of Eve – could this be Esau's *mamm*? She had followed Annie by the creek, she had been unwell, she had arrived in Faith's Creek unexpectedly, and by her attire – trousers covered by a long baggy top – she was not of the Amish faith. But it was the way she looked at Esau that was enough to convince Annie her visit to the flower store was no coincidence. She could not keep her eyes off the *boppli*, and Annie smiled at her, not wanting to upset her by mentioning the incident by the creek.

"What a beautiful *boppli*," Eve said.

"You can hold him if you like. I can't arrange flowers with him in my arms. I'd have to put him down in his basket if not," Annie replied.

Eve looked suddenly uncertain, but Annie held Esau out to her, and she took him, cradling him gently in her arms and smiling at him.

"He's just perfect," she exclaimed.

Annie smiled, the fear now replaced with something else, something she couldn't quite put her fingers on. "Isn't he just?" she said, beginning to take stems of white flowers from various vases and arrange them into a bouquet.

"You've got such a nice store here," Marshall said, looking around him.

"That's kind of you to say. I've worked hard on it. It wasn't easy at first. I didn't know if anyone in Faith's Creek would want to buy cut flowers. But it seems they do. I'm run off my feet with orders for bouquets, and a lot of the *Englischer* families come too. This week I've had a rush with those wanting to leave wreaths on graves for anniversaries. Flowers set the tone for so many occasions, don't you think?" she said, glancing at Eve, who was gazing down at Esau, who now slept in her arms.

"That's very true. I just grow vegetables, as I told you. But you can't say "happy anniversary" with a carrot or a leek, can you?" Marshall said, laughing, as Annie finished making up the bouquet.

She smiled at him and shook her head. "*Nee*, I don't think I'd appreciate a pumpkin on my birthday," she replied.

"You're... not betrothed, then," he said, his tone changing.

Annie shook her head. "*Nee*. I came here from Oregon after my *mamm* died. I wanted a fresh start, I suppose. But that didn't entail getting married. Not in Oregon, at least," she replied, glancing up at him and smiling.

He blushed, and Annie handed over the bouquet of white flowers, which she had wrapped in cellophane and pink tissue paper and tied with a red ribbon. They looked very pretty, and now she turned back to Eve, who was still cradling Esau in her arms as though she had no intention of ever letting him go.

"We'd better go, Eve," Marshall said.

His cousin looked up in surprise. "Oh, already?" she said.

"We can't stay all day," he replied.

Annie went over to Eve, holding out her arms, as Eve reluctantly handed Esau back to her. As she looked at Eve and down at Esau, Annie was surprised at the resemblance between the two. Previously, Annie would have dismissed those who made claims to see a resemblance between a parent and a *boppli* – all babies looked the same, at least in Annie's opinion – but in the face of Eve, she caught a glimpse of Esau, and vice versa. It was the dimple in the chin, and the eyes – the same eyes. It was all she could do not to gasp at the sight.

"You're welcome to come back anytime," Annie said, as Marshall opened the store door for his sister.

"*Denke* – you've been very kind," he said, and Annie smiled at him.

"Well, you're just across the square at the mercantile. Don't be a stranger," she said, as Marshall and Eve left the store.

Annie had been glad to see the mercantile store clerk again. He had a certain way about him – it was as though he was embarrassed, even as this was the second time he had found an excuse to visit her at the flower store. He was certainly handsome, and Annie was only too glad to have made his acquaintance. She admired him for the way he was taking such obvious care of his cousin, but Annie could not rid herself of the suspicion as to Eve's true identity.

"I think we might've found your *mamm*, Esau," she said out loud, smiling down at the *boppli* in her arms, and wondering what to do next.

CHAPTER THIRTEEN

*A*nnie worked for the rest of the morning. She made up the bouquets and the wreaths, ensuring everything was as her customers had asked. She took delivery of fresh stock, removing dead heads and stripping off the leaves, before placing the new blooms in fresh water. The window display was rearranged, and when Annie eventually sat down, it was gone one o'clock. But whilst her jobs had kept her busy, her mind had been elsewhere. Annie could not stop thinking about the possibility of Eve being Esau's *mamm*. The resemblance was uncanny, and more than that, the bond was evident. Esau had fallen asleep in Eve's arms, and when it came time for them to leave, she had not wanted to let him go.

But how to approach it? There's still the question of why she left him in the first place, Annie thought to herself, as she lifted Esau from his basket to give him a bottle of warm milk.

Knowing she could not keep her suspicions to herself, Annie finished feeding Esau before putting on her shawl and closing the store. She wanted a second opinion, and with Esau in a sling around her shoulders, she walked across the market square in the direction of Bishop Beiler's house.

"Are you shutting up for the day?" Monica called out.

"*Nee,* I'll be back soon. If anyone comes, would you tell them I won't be long?" Annie called back.

Monica nodded and waved to her. Annie was grateful for new friends. Monica had been amongst the first to welcome her to Faith's Creek, and she had proved a trusted confidante in the matter of Esau and the mystery surrounding him. Annie was relieved to see Sarah Beiler in the garden of the Bishop's house. She was cutting chrysanthemums, and she looked up as Annie approached and smiled.

"Don't worry, I won't do you out of business with these. But I do love chrysanthemums, don't you?" Sarah said.

"They're lovely. You've got some pretty colors here. I'll have to buy mine from you instead of the wholesaler," Annie replied, laughing, as Sarah took up her basket of cut flowers and beckoned Annie to follow her.

"Come in, it's *gut* to see you – and *boppli* Esau. I'll make us some coffee, and cut a slice of cake. It's the special coconut one from the Miller's bakery," Sarah said, and she led Annie into the house.

The parlor was comfortably furnished, and Annie could hear the voice of Bishop Beiler coming from the study. It sounded like he was practicing his preaching for the coming Sunday, his clear, booming voice extolling the virtues of the *gut* Samaritan.

"Please, don't go to any trouble. But I had to talk to you about Esau," Annie said, as she sat down on a comfortable chair by the stove and cradled him in her arms.

Sarah was making the coffee, and she looked up at Annie and smiled at her reassuringly. "It's all right, you can talk to me about anything. Is something troubling you?" she asked.

Annie shook her head. "There's nothing wrong with Esau, it's just... I think I might know who the *mamm* is."

Sarah looked at her in surprise, and Annie recounted the story of her walk with Esau by the creek and how she had encountered the same woman who had turned out to be Marshall's cousin, Eve.

"And she held him in the flower store?" Sarah asked as Annie finished her story.

"That's right, and it wasn't just the appearance that was the same. There was a bond between them. I can't quite explain it," Annie replied.

Sarah poured her a cup of coffee and sat down opposite her next to the stove. She was silent for a moment, pondering Annie's words.

"It makes sense, doesn't it... she arrived around the same time Esau did. She's been unwell, withdrawn into herself, and now this... it's not beyond the realm of possibility. Was she reluctant to go with Marshall once it was time to leave?" Sarah asked.

Annie nodded. "Very much so. She didn't want to hand him back, that was certain," Annie replied.

The more she thought about it, the more she was convinced she was right. But the question remained – what were they to do about their suspicion? If Eve did not want to reveal herself as Esau's *mamm*, then there was nothing they could do about it. They could not force her to take responsibility, even as Annie was certain she sensed regret in Eve's eyes at the sight of Esau, and a reluctance to hand him back.

"We don't know for certain. It's a suspicion, but a well-founded one. Do you think Marshall suspects anything?" Sarah asked.

Annie took a sip of coffee and shook her head. Marshall – as kind and caring as he was – appeared entirely oblivious to his cousin's demeanor towards Esau. He had brought her to the flower store to cheer her up – that was all it seemed, and there had been no ulterior motive on his part.

"I don't think so. I think he was just glad Eve wasn't missing as they feared. He brought her to the flower store as a way to distract her. I don't think he'd realize if she'd had a *boppli*. But Doctor Yoder would – that's why she didn't want to be examined. She was scared of being found out... it makes sense, doesn't it?" Annie said.

Sarah nodded. "It makes perfect sense, Annie. Well done, it can't have been easy for you. But we need to be careful about what happens next. Eve might not be ready for the responsibility of a *boppli*. That's why she gave him up. She's clearly torn between the two – she wants to be a part of Esau's life, but she can't admit it. She'll feel guilty for abandoning him, even as she tries to make amends now," Sarah replied.

Annie nodded. She knew there was a danger in all of this. Eve had abandoned her *boppli* to strangers. She had not been thinking properly, and now, it seemed she was taking a risk in following Annie and coming to visit Esau at the flower shop.

"But what should I do? Should I ask her directly? Or should I wait for her to make the first move? I don't even know for certain if she's the *mamm*," Annie said.

Sarah thought for a moment. "All you can do is wait. She might not be ready to reveal it yet. Let her trust you first. I'm sure it's all right for her to come to the flower store with Marshall. You'd be there all the time. You're in control of this, Annie. I'll visit Marshall's *mamm*. Linda used to be part of our quilting circle. I'll raise our suspicions with her – she might've been thinking the same thing," Sarah said.

Annie was relieved to have shared her fears with Sarah. It was hard bearing the brunt of responsibility, and the Bishop's *fraa* had helped her considerably simply by listening. Having finished her coffee, and a slice of moist and delicious cake, she thanked Sarah and returned to the flower store. Monica was still serving customers at her stall, and she waved to Annie as she approached.

"You had a couple of inquiries, and you just missed Marshall's cousin – I think it was. I told her you'd be back soon, and she said she'll call again," Monica said.

Annie wanted to see Eve again. She wanted to talk to her when Marshall was not there. If only she could hear her tell the truth, it would make everything easier. Annie was convinced Eve was Esau's *mamm*, and now she wanted only to do what was best for each of them.

"That's kind of you, Monica, *denke*," Annie replied.

She opened up the store, finding everything as she had left it. Esau was growing restless in the sling, and she took him out of it, cradling him in her arms and placing him in the basket, which she placed amidst the vases of flowers. The scent appeared to soothe him, and Annie smiled down at him, filled with love for the *boppli* she had tried her best to take care of.

"I think I know who your *mamm* is. But I'm going to miss you so much," she said, placing her finger on the *boppli's* lips as he blew bubbles and gurgled.

She left him to fall asleep in the basket, and made her way into the storeroom, ready to tackle the myriad of jobs neglected that day. She was just selecting a color of ribbon to tie a bunch of roses together when the bell above the door jangled.

"Just a moment," she called out before the bell jangled once again.

Annie rolled her eyes – people were so impatient for service. She had learned that since opening her store – people could be rude. She shook her head, putting down the piece of ribbon on the worktop in the storeroom and stepping out to the front to select the flowers she needed for the bouquet.

"I think perhaps some gerberas and verbena," she thought to herself, but as she glanced across at the basket amidst the vases of flowers, a terrible sight met her eyes – Esau was gone.

CHAPTER FOURTEEN

"*I* just can't stop thinking about those peanut butter squares. It's the way she gets them so soft and squidgy," Joseph Peters said, pausing with a tin of paint in his hand to look wistfully up into the distance, as though he was picturing a plate of the longed-for confectionary in front of him.

Marshall laughed. They were stacking tins of paint in the window of the mercantile, and now he climbed down from his stepladder to unbox the next set of colors.

"Should I tell my *mamm* you're wanting to marry her? You'd get peanut butter squares every day if you did," he said, shaking his head.

"I'd seriously consider it, I've... oh, what's going on over there?" Joseph replied.

Marshall turned to look. Joseph was pointing across the market square to where a commotion was taking place outside the flower store. He could see Annie and Monica there, each pointing in different directions, as others gathered around them.

"I'd better go and see what's happening," Marshall said, and without a second thought to the tins of paint, he hurried out of the store and across the market square to where Annie and the others were gathered.

"I don't know which way they've gone. I didn't see anything," Monica was saying.

"We need to spread out. They can't have gone far," Annie replied, and now she looked up at Marshall with an anxious expression on her face.

"What's happened?" he asked.

"It's Esau – someone's taken him from the flower store, and I think I know who it might be," she said.

Marshall was confused, even as he stared at her in astonishment. A *kinnernapping*? In Faith's Creek. Such a thing was unheard of, and it seemed the whole community was coming out to help in the search, as news spread of Esau's disappearance.

"But... who?" he asked.

Annie looked him straight in the eye. "I think it's Eve. I think she's Esau's *mamm*," she replied.

Marshall was too shocked to take this in. Eve could not possibly be Esau's *mamm*. It did not make sense. "But... it... she can't be," he stammered.

"Are you going to help look for the *boppli*, or not?" Monica interjected, and Marshall was temporarily returned to his senses.

"Of course... I'll do anything to help. What about the creek? It's quiet down there. Whoever has Esau might be hiding there," he replied, for he still could not believe his cousin was responsible.

"We'll search there, the rest of you spread out around the market square. Check the other stores, knock on doors, let everyone know the *boppli's* missing," Annie called out, and she hurried across the square, followed by Marshall, who had to run to keep up.

"But why do you think it's Eve that's got the *boppli*?" he asked, as they came to the path leading down to the creek.

"Isn't it obvious? Didn't you see the way she looked at him at the flower store when she was holding him?" Annie replied, turning to Marshall with an exasperated look on her face.

To Marshall's embarrassment, he had not noticed the way his cousin had looked at Esau. He had been too busy looking at Annie to notice anything else. There had been *nee* suggestion Eve had given birth to a *boppli*, even as Marshall had to admit, he would not know the signs if she had done so. Of course, if he thought about it, she stayed in bed a lot and she always wore baggy clothes. When she came the last time, she had worn jeans and a t-shirt so popular amongst the *Englischers*.

"I... I don't know, I suppose it could be her," he replied, realizing how little he knew about his cousin.

She had come from Philadelphia with no indication of why or what had happened to her. They had believed her when she had said things had been difficult. The arrival of a *boppli* would certainly have been a difficulty, as much as Marshall hated to think of his cousin suffering such an ordeal alone.

"She turns up out of nowhere, she won't let Doctor Yoder examine her, she looks like Esau – the dimple on her chin – and then she finds a reason to come to the flower store and hold the *boppli* herself. I saw how she looked. Can't you understand?" Annie exclaimed.

Marshall had not meant to make her angry. He could see the upset in her voice. She was desperate to find Esau, and now they made their way along the path by the creek, desperately searching for any sign of Eve and the *boppli*. Annie's words made sense, and Marshall felt foolish for not having recognized the signs.

"I'm sorry... I just didn't expect it, that's all. We really know so little about her. I didn't realize what was going on," he said, shaking his head.

Annie turned to him and sighed. "It's not always obvious. But I saw her – down here one afternoon. She'd followed me. I didn't know it was Eve at the time, but when the two of you came to the flower store that afternoon, I recognized her. I think she was following me out of curiosity, and perhaps I was foolish to allow her to hold the *boppli*. It must've raised all sorts of feelings in her," Annie replied.

Marshall felt terribly sorry for Eve – if it was true, and she was Esau's *mamm*, she had suffered in silence, and he and his *mamm* had done nothing to help her. He was about to admit as much when, up ahead, he saw her, sitting by the water's edge, cradling Esau in her arms.

"Eve, what are you doing?" he called out, as they hurried towards her.

"I'm with my *boppli*," Eve replied, rising to her feet, and holding Esau close as she looked fearfully from Marshall to Annie and back.

"Is that the truth, Eve?" Marshall asked, taking a step forward.

His cousin nodded. "He's mine. I won't let him go," she replied, even as Esau began to cry.

"It's all right, Eve. No one's going to hurt you. We just want what's best for the *boppli*," Annie said, as she, too, took a step forward.

"Please... he's mine. I made a mistake. I made a terrible mistake," Eve exclaimed, as tears welled up in her eyes.

"Then make it better," Marshall replied, as Annie held out her hands imploringly, and Marshall prayed his cousin would not do something foolish.

CHAPTER FIFTEEN

*I*t had not surprised Annie to have her suspicions confirmed. Ever since she had seen Eve holding Esau in the flower store, she had known Marshall's cousin was the *mamm*. What she did not know – what no one except Eve knew – was the set of circumstances that had led to the *boppli* being left amongst the vases in the flower store window.

Eve was crying, and so was Esau, and she handed the *boppli* to Annie, who shushed him.

"It's all right, you're safe – you're both safe," she said, smiling at Eve, for she could not be angry with her.

Annie's overall feeling was of relief. She had prayed to *Gott* for Esau's deliverance, and now she had found him safe and sound in his *mamm's* arms.

"But... I don't understand what happened? How did you prevent anyone from knowing?" Marshall asked.

"Well... they did know. Back in Philadelphia, they did. That's why I was let go from my waitressing job. They didn't want a pregnant teenager serving milkshakes. I didn't know what else to do. I gave birth at this woman's place, but my landlord didn't want a baby in the house. He gave me notice. I had $100 to my name. Enough to pay what I owed and take the greyhound bus here to Faith's Creek. I knew what you'd say if I turned up on the doorstep with a baby. I didn't want to leave him, I really didn't," Eve said, looking up at Marshall, who, to his credit, put his arm around her and kissed her head.

"*Nee* one's angry with you, Eve. We're just relieved you're all right, and that Esau's all right. Though I suppose you had a different name for him," Marshall said.

Eve shook her head. "I didn't know what to call him. I kept changing my mind. But I like Esau, it's... lovely. I'm so grateful to you, Annie," Eve said, looking up at Annie and smiling.

"I did what I felt was right. You left him with me for a reason, and I wanted to do my best for him," Annie replied.

She still did not know why Eve had chosen her, but she was grateful to have played a small part in the story, as hard as she knew it would be to give him up, if that was what Eve wanted.

"I saw you through the window of the flower store. It was just a feeling I had – a feeling you'd be the right person to take care of Esau. I don't know why I felt like that, but I was right, wasn't I?" Eve replied.

Annie looked down at the *boppli* in her arms and smiled. She would not have had it any other way. She had come to love Esau as her own, and she felt certain *Gott* had brought the two of them together for a reason.

"I'm glad to have been a part of Esau's story. Even just a small part," she replied.

"You're more than that. You went above and beyond to help him – and to help Eve," Marshall said.

"I'm sorry I snapped at you earlier," Annie said.

Marshall only laughed and shook his head. "You don't need to apologize. I don't blame you – I was a little slow on the uptake. I'm just glad... well, Eve, what do you want to happen now? You're Esau's *mamm*, but... do you want to be?" he asked.

This was the same question Annie was curious to know the answer to. Eve had taken Esau for a reason – had she come to regret what she had done? Eve took a deep breath and wiped the tears from her eyes. She looked at Esau, lying asleep in Annie's arms, and smiled.

"I regretted leaving him in the flower store. I regretted it as soon as I did it. That's why I followed you down here to the creek that afternoon. I wasn't sure what to do. I didn't have the courage to tell you the truth, but I couldn't stay away from him, either. When I held him in the flower store that afternoon, my heart melted. I remembered what it felt like the first time I held him. I didn't want to let him go," she said, shaking her head.

"I can help you," Annie replied.

She had not thought through the implications of what she was saying, but she knew she wanted to be a part of Esau's life. She loved him, and she would always love him, whether he went with Eve, or stayed with her.

Eve looked at her in surprise. "Do you mean it?" she asked.

Annie nodded. "I know it won't be easy. But we can manage, I'm sure. You take him now, and I'll come to help you," Annie said.

Tears welled up in her eyes, even as she knew she was doing the right thing. Esau belonged with his *mamm*, but Eve now looked uncertain.

"I... I don't know. What's my aunt going to say?" she said, glancing at Marshall, who shook his head.

"She's going to be surprised, that's for certain. But we can explain. She'll understand," he said, holding out his hand to Eve, who nodded and took a deep breath.

"All right, but only if Annie comes, too," she replied, turning to Annie, who nodded.

"I'll come. I don't mind," she said.

"We don't want to inconvenience you," Marshall said.

It was not an inconvenience. Annie was only too happy to help – she wanted to help – and now she handed Esau to Eve, who cradled him in her arms and smiled.

"You're so beautiful, aren't you? I just couldn't believe it when I saw him for the first time. The life I'd made," she said.

Annie still had so many questions, but she held back, allowing Eve to bond with Esau, who had now opened his eyes and was looking up at her, gurgling and blowing bubbles. They made their way back up the path from the creek, taking a route so they could let people know that he had been found. They said nothing else for now, but word would soon spread, and people could stop looking and relax.

"I want to get Eve home," Marshall said, falling back a few steps behind his cousin so as to talk to Annie.

"She's going to need a lot of support," Annie replied, and Marshall nodded.

"I know, and I'm so grateful to you for what you've done. I thought you'd be angry with her – you had every right to be angry with her," he said, but Annie shook her head.

She was not angry with Eve. She could only imagine how difficult it must have been for her to give up her son and leave him in the flower shop. It was only right for them to be reunited, and Annie was glad to have played her part in doing so.

"I'm not angry, not at all. She's suffered a great deal, and I'm just glad she's all right. She's done the right thing, and Esau has his *mamm* back," Annie replied.

Her feelings were mixed, but she knew she had played her part as *Gott* had intended. It was not long before they reached Marshall's house, with its neat rows of vegetables growing in the garden.

"I'm afraid there aren't any flowers," Marshall said.

Annie was impressed. "I can grow flowers, you can grow vegetables. We could sell them together," she said.

Marshall smiled. "It's a nice idea," he said.

Annie shook her head. "I'm being serious. I've been thinking of ways to expand the business," she replied.

Just then, the door to the house opened, and Linda appeared, looking astonished at the sight of Eve holding the *boppli*. "Eve? What's going on?"

"I think we should come inside and talk," Marshall replied, and that was just what they did.

To say Linda was surprised would be an understatement, but she listened patiently to the explanation. Annie, too, learned the answers to her questions, as Eve explained how she had come to be with child and all alone in Philadelphia.

"I thought he loved me. He told me he loved me. And then he went off with that... I can't even say her name. It broke my heart, and then I discovered I was pregnant. I didn't know what to do. I thought I could make a go of things on my own, but... I just couldn't," Eve said.

After she had finished her explanation, Linda put her arms around her and kissed her. "I wish you'd just told us the truth, Eve. We could've helped you. We would've helped you. But we *can* help you now," she said.

Eve sniffed and nodded. "I'm sorry, I just didn't know what to do," she said, glancing at Annie.

"You did what you thought was best. You wanted to help Esau. We understand," she said, glancing at the *boppli*, asleep in his *mamm's* arms. There was a little pang of sadness in her heart but there was also a feeling that this was right.

"And we need to be grateful to you above anyone, Annie. *Denke* – from the bottom of my heart, *denke*," Linda said.

"I'm just glad I could help," she replied, knowing she had done just what her own *mamm* had always taught her, and followed her heart which was the prompting of *Gott*.

CHAPTER SIXTEEN

*I*t had felt strange for Annie to return home alone that afternoon. Word of Esau being found had spread quickly, and the whole community was relieved to hear he was safe, even as there was some surprise as to the identity of his *mamm*.

"At least you don't have the responsibility now, do you?" Monica had said after Annie had explained everything that had happened by the creek, and how Eve had been reunited with her son.

"I didn't mind the responsibility. I'm going to miss him," Annie said.

It had not taken long for her to grow used to having Esau as part of her life. She had bonded with him and grown to love him. The cottage now felt empty, and Annie had not known what to do with her evening alone. She was still surrounded by the well-meaning gifts of those in the community who had wanted to help – there were enough *boppli* clothes to open a store, and piles of diapers stacked around the parlor. Annie had not stopped thinking about Esau all night long, and whilst she knew he was in the right place, it did not stop her from missing him terribly.

"You can't cling to memories," she had told herself, as she opened the flower store the next morning.

But in her work that day, Annie felt she had lost something of her passion. Her thoughts were distracted, and she kept expecting to be disturbed by the cries of a *boppli*. But the store was quiet, and she had no customers all morning. At noon, Annie retreated to the storeroom, sorting out neglected boxes of deliveries, and sighing to herself at the thought of now being alone once again.

"But I'm a strong person. I'll manage," she told herself, just as the bell above the store door jangled.

Annie looked out of the storeroom to find Sarah Beiler and several other women from the quilting circle standing in front of the counter.

"We wanted to make sure you were all right," Sarah said, as Annie emerged to serve them.

She nodded, trying not to show her emotions, for she did not wish to be regarded as an object of pity.

"I'm all right. I've got plenty of work to do, and..." she replied, fighting back the tears.

Sarah came to put her arm around her, and the other women – Susanna, Anna, and Lavinia – made sympathetic noises.

"It's all right, Annie. You did a wonderful job of taking care of Esau. This community owes you a debt of gratitude. But it's not the end of your involvement with him," Sarah said.

Annie looked up at her in surprise. "I... I don't understand?" she said, just as the bell above the door jangled once again.

Annie turned, and to her surprise, she found Marshall standing in front of the counter. He smiled at her. "I've come to buy some flowers," he said.

Annie smiled. "That's usually why people come to a flower store," she replied.

SARAH MILLER & IRENE GLICK

Marshall blushed, it made him even more handsome and she noticed that the women from the quilting circle had stepped back as if they were expecting something. There was expectation on their faces.

"I'm not sure what to choose, though. Do you have a favorite flower?" he asked.

Annie smiled. No one had ever asked her what her favorite flower was, and now she looked around at the vases, pondering her answer.

"I... I like peonies. They're so blowsy, aren't they?" she said, her eyes falling on the vase of pink peonies in full bloom.

"Then I'll take a dozen of them," Marshall said.

Annie assumed they were for Eve, and she took the blooms from the vase and wrapped them in cellophane and tissue paper, tying them with a pink bow. Marshall took them, handing over the money, and then, to Annie's immense surprise, he handed them back.

"Oh, is something wrong?" she asked.

He smiled and looked around at the women's faces. They were practically grinning, what was going on?

"*Nee*," he said.

"But... aren't they for Eve?" she asked.

Marshall shook his head. "*Nee...* they're for you. I wanted to thank you for everything you've done – for Esau, for Eve, for all of us," he said.

A tear rolled down Annie's cheek, and she breathed in the scent of the peonies, smiling at Marshall, as the members of the quilting circle slipped silently out of the store.

"That's very kind of you. I was glad to help," Annie replied.

"But you did more than help. You gave Eve a second chance, there was no judgment when you found out, no condemnation. That's priceless. She needed that. She needed someone to trust her. It's going to take time, but she'll make a wonderful *mamm*," Marshall replied.

"I know she will. But... will she stay in Faith's Creek?" Annie asked.

She had been wondering as to this question and praying she would not entirely lose Esau, even as she knew things now had to be very different.

"She's going to stay, and... well, she wants to come back to the faith. It's because of you, Annie. She saw your example, your calling from *Gott*," Marshall replied.

Annie was taken aback. She had not believed herself to be acting out any sort of moral example. She had done what her heart had told her to do. That was all.

"Well... I'm so pleased to hear it. That's wonderful news," she exclaimed.

Marshall smiled. "She's got a lot to learn. She didn't grow up in the faith or learn anything of scripture or tradition as a *kinner*. But she wants to learn, and she wants to do right by Esau. She wants you to be a part of his life. A significant part. And so do I..." Marshall said.

Annie smiled. She could think of nothing she wanted more than to do just that – to be a part of Esau's life and to help Eve in any way she could. But it was Marshall's final words which brought a lump to her throat.

"You do?" she asked.

He nodded. "Look... I'm not very *gut* at this. I've wanted to speak to you ever since I first saw you across the market square. I couldn't pluck up the courage to do so, the ladies had to give me a little push. When I first came to buy the flowers, I wanted to say more... I'm not making much sense, am I?" he said, sighing and shaking his head.

He looked embarrassed, but Annie set down the bunch of peonies and reached out to take his hand in hers.

"I think I know what you're saying. And the flowers say what words can't. I'm so glad I could be a part of Esau's life, and I'm so glad it allowed the two of us to meet. I'd noticed you, too. I'd been trying to find an excuse to come to the mercantile store, but there wasn't anything I needed. I know as much about what you sell as you know about flowers," she said, laughing, as Marshall smiled and shook his head.

"Well... perhaps we could start again if you'd like that," he said.

Annie nodded. "I'd like that very much. What did you have in mind?" she asked.

His cheeks flushed even more. "Would you like to come for dinner this evening? My *mamm's* an excellent cook, and you could help Eve bathe Esau and get him ready for bed. Come as soon as you've closed up the store. I can show you the vegetable patch, too. Were you serious about us selling vegetables?" he said.

Annie chuckled as the words streamed out of him with *nee* room for her to answer.

"That sounds delightful, and *jah*, I was. I think it's about time I branched out. Flowers and vegetables. I like the sound of it," she replied, and smiling at Marshall, she took up the bunch of peonies, grateful to him for what he had done, and excited at the prospect of what the future held.

EPILOGUE

*I*t was six months later, and Annie was looking around the flower store with a satisfied look on her face.

"I think we've done it, Eve," she said, glancing at Marshall's cousin, who had just finished tying the final ribbon on the last bouquet they had to make.

"Is this all right, Annie? I want to get it just right." Eve held up the bouquet – a mixture of pink begonias and red roses.

It looked very pretty, and Annie was impressed by how far Eve had come in her skills as a flower arranger since she had started working in the flower store.

"They look perfect," she said, just as the cry of a *boppli* filled the air.

"And right on cue, our little friend wakes up," Eve said.

Esau was in a crib made by Marshall for the shop. He came with them to work each day, sleeping, then waking, and often filling the store with his cries. Annie and Eve took it in turns to see to him, and there was always a steady stream of customers eager for news of the blossoming *boppli*. In their spare time, they looked after Esau or Annie would coach Eve on the *Ordnung*. She was a quick learner and was already loved by many in the district. Annie saw *nee* problem if and when she wanted to commit.

"I think he's hungry. I'll feed him," Eve said, retreating to the storeroom.

"And look who's coming to see us," Eve said, pointing out of the store window and across the market square to where Marshall was hurrying towards them.

"He looks flustered. It must be about the wedding," Annie said, smiling as Marshall entered the store.

"Celery," he exclaimed, and Annie looked at him in surprise.

He had proposed to her two months previously. For a moment her mind went back to that proposal. Eve had looked after the store while he took her for a picnic down by the creek. For the first time in a while, he had been nervous and his sentences ran into each other making his words garbled, as always happened when he was worried about something.

The picnic was wonderful, with fried chicken and salad and an apple pie and cream. She imagined either Eve or Linda, his mamm, had prepared it.

He spread the blanket on the ground near the river and beneath the shade of a tree. His fingers were shaking as he put the food before them.

"What is it?" she had asked and for a moment, she was afraid. What if he was tired of her?

Marshall sat before her and took her hands in his. They looked so small in his large manly workman's hands but it felt right. He looked down and then up at her. His cheeks were crimson and his adam's apple was bobbing in his throat as he swallowed.

"Marshall, you're making me nervous," she said.

"Nee, don't be." He swallowed again. "I love you; I have loved you for a long while and I want us to be together

forever, I want Gott to know how much I love you; will you marry me?"

Annie sat for a few moments as her mind followed the long stream of words. It took her a while to get through it all and she could see the worry on his face. He thought her delay was hesitancy, but it was not. She grabbed his cheeks and pulled him to her placing a kiss on his lips.

She pulled back, the biggest grin ever on her face.

"Is that a jah?" he had asked.

"I love you too, you big fool," she had said. "Of course, it is a jah. I can't wait to be your fraa. After all, then Esau will be my relative." She winked at him and he had pulled her into his arms. It was a wonderful day and she knew she would never forget it.

"Are you listening?" he asked.

Annie was pulled back to the present. "Humm?" she asked.

"I said I'm so happy."

"Me too, I love you so much and was just remembering your proposal. It was wonderful."

"Ha, I doubt it. I bet I stumbled and spoke so fast you couldn't understand me."

"I got there," she said.

The wedding was just two days away. It was not usual for the Amish to have flowers at a wedding, but Annie had insisted, and the bouquets they had made that morning were for her and Eve to carry as they entered the barn where the ceremony was to take place.

"What about celery?" Eve asked.

"It's a tradition, isn't it? The bride's *mamm* plants celery as a sign of the wedding about to take place. I hadn't thought about it. But we can plant it together, can't we? In memory of your *mamm*," Marshall said, smiling at Annie as she laughed and shook her head.

"I don't think it matters," she replied, but Marshall was adamant.

He had wanted to do everything properly, and it seemed the planting of the celery was essential to their future happiness.

"You two go and plant it in the vegetable garden. Take Esau with you, and I'll finish up here – I just need to put the bouquets in water," Eve said, having quickly given Esau his feed.

Annie and Marshall set off with the *boppli* towards Marshall's house – and the home that would soon be Annie's, too.

"I didn't know anything about planting celery before a wedding," Annie said, as they carried the basket, containing Esau, between them.

"It's for the decorations, and some of the dishes at the meal. We'll have to pick some from the crop I've already got. But I like the idea of planting it together, too. We're sewing seeds for the future," Marshall said, as they came in sight of the house and garden.

Annie liked the idea, too. She was only too glad to be sewing seeds for their future, and if it had not been for the planting of so many other seeds, that future might never have come. Great things could come from the smallest seed, and Annie could only feel happy at the thought of seeing their lives together grow.

"I wonder what those seeds are going to grow into – we've got one right here," Annie said, looking down at Esau and smiling.

"Seeds need nurturing, watering, care, attention... growing a garden takes time. But I think we've got the patience for it," Marshall replied, smiling at Annie, who nodded.

"Then let's see how it grows," she replied, as she looked forward to everything that was to come, and all the future held.

If you enjoyed this book you will love A Love to Heal her Heart

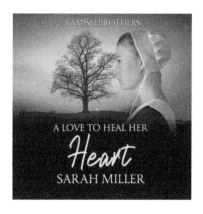

AMISH OF FAITH'S CREEK 4 BOOK BOX SET – PREVIEW

* * *

"I have told you these things,
so that in me you may have peace.
In this world you will have trouble.
But take heart!
I have overcome the world."
- John 16:3

* * *

A cool breeze lifted the ties of her bonnet and let them fall gently against her neck. Roseanna Wagler brushed the tie away absently and closed her eyes. The breeze felt good and clean with the scent of grass as she moved through the field. It eased the weight from her shoulders and cooled the sweat on her brow. Today was a perfect day to be working in the meadow. The sort of day she lived for and there was plenty of work to be done.

Opening her eyes, she glanced across the land. How she loved this view. The vista of green spread out before her like *Gott's* perfect patchwork. There were fields of grass, dotted with black and white Friesian cattle. As she watched, she could almost smell their earthy scent and hear their moos as they came in for milking.

Her eyes moved across to the horses, bays, the occasional gray, and the big chestnut Dutch horses that the landscape and the Amish were famous for. Then there were the beautiful mixed colors of corn spread out before her along with all varieties of potatoes, vegetables, and the river in the distance. It was perfect, peaceful, and filled her with joy and only a touch of loneliness.

Wiggling her bare toes in the earth she lowered her head and looked at their own fields. It was good fertile soil and the crop would be heavy this year. The barley was not quite turning. The ears were still upright and the color still green. As it ripened the nutty scent would increase, but for now, it was sweet and barely detectable. This was the ideal time to walk between the rows to pluck out the weeds. So why was she feeling guilty?

The sound of hooves traveling on gravel carried across the field and her eyes were drawn to the buggy. The horse was trotting fast. It looked like *Daed* was worried. Maybe she should have gone with them. Roseanna's hand reached down and wrapped around the wild oats. With a quick pull, she ripped out the weed and placed it in her basket while walking along the row without needing to look. Up ahead a large patch of weeds was choking the barley.

No, she was right to stay.

The work needed doing and *bopplis* were born every day. There was nothing special about this birth. Nothing that needed her to be there more than she was needed in the fields. It promised to be a good crop. To provide them with an income to keep up with the rent and tide them over the winter. It would be careless to leave it unattended just to visit with her sister-in-law. Just to take her to the hospital. Anyway, the buggy would be crowded enough.

Quickly her hands reached for another weed as her eyes followed the buggy. It was fading into the distance now and the pace had not slowed. In fact, she couldn't be sure at this distance, but she thought the horse was cantering. A hand seemed to clench onto her gut and squeeze the air from her lungs.

Should she have gone?

Mary would be fine. So why did she worry? Her brother already had one child and Mary had shown no problems throughout this pregnancy. Yet *Daed* had been different this morning. Something about the look in his eyes made Rose wonder if she should have gone with them. Absently she reached for the weeds and plucked them from the field. *Gott* would take care of her family. He would see that all was right with the world. The way He sent the rain and the sunshine... but what about the weeds? He sent those too and without help, they would swamp the fields and smother the barley. If she did not tend the field, the harvest would be poor. Maybe it was the same with *kinner*. If you did not attend the birth, then things got out of hand. But her brother, David was there with her *daed*. They did not need her.

From across the field, the sound of a young girls' laughter floated on the breeze. Katie could always find something to laugh at. Right now she would be tending to Atlee, her brother's and Mary's two-year-old son. As another peel of laughter floated towards her, guilt flooded her stomach with bile. Katie was only eleven and yet she had taken it upon herself to look after Atlee. Rose ripped at the weeds, pulling them out as fast as she could and trying to blot out the thought of her sister doing all the work. No, that was wrong. Katie and her twin Lydia did the majority of the housework, the cooking, cleaning, and washing. They baked and roasted and kept the house as clean as it had been before their *mamm* deserted them. But they never milked the cow or chopped wood. They never plowed the fields or harvested the corn. Rose did those so her sisters didn't have to. She took on more of the farm as her *daed* got older. It had never been a burden. Reach and pull, reach and pull. The weeds grasped onto the dry soil and each time it seemed harder to pull them loose. It was as if they were fighting her. As if they defied her and wanted her to know she should not be here.

A cry rang across the field and Rose stopped. The sound of a child in pain filled her with despair. It took her back to the day their mother left. The sound of her sister's crying still haunted her dreams... almost as much as the look in her *daed's* eyes. Katie and Lydia were just six years old. Roseanna had been fifteen, almost an adult, and it had fallen on her to become the woman of the house.

A cut formed on her hand as it slipped across a ryegrass stalk. The weed seemed to wave before her, defiantly happy that it managed to draw blood. She bent down and wrapped her fingers around it pulling once more. For a second the tough grass held firm and tears formed in her eyes. How could she go on? Then the grass came loose and she almost fell backward.

This was her place. The crying from the field's headland had stopped. As always Katie had eased the child's tears. Now she would be bouncing little Atlee on her knee. Cooing and chuckling with him. Making him forget his *mamm* was not there. It had been just the same when their *mamm* left. Katie had taken over. She had looked after so much even though she was so young. She had held her sisters and soothed away their tears. While they clung to her, her little face filled with resolve as she dried her tears, Rose had felt so awkward. It should have been her doing those things but she didn't feel like an adult. All she wanted to do was drop to her knees and let Katie hold her. Then she had fled to the stables and watched the horses and the chickens. They had no worries, no stresses and they went about their day as if *Gott* provided everything for them. It had been a hard lesson. To know that she had to *let go and let Gott,* but she could not do it. On the outside, she carried on, but inside she was betrayed and hurt and she wanted to scream at *Gott* that it was not fair.

Gradually the years passed, but she never got over the hurt. It was like armor and she wore it to protect her from getting too close. If you let no one in, no one could betray you.

All the time Katie had been so small and yet so in control. Instead of crying, she helped others. At first, Rose thought of her as a child playing house but that changed. Soon she was so proficient. In a few years, she had taken over the cooking from Rose. Their meals had changed from burnt offerings to good, healthy, and tasty food. Rose had fled the house and found solace on the farm. The work was hard and yet easier... for her at least. It stopped her thinking, stopped her worrying, and kept her busy. There was no need to worry about anyone else when she worked the fields. No need to worry who she would hurt, or who would leave, or anything like that. The work just was, and she was out in *Gott's* glorious sunshine.

"You need to marry," *Daed* had said just last week.

Rose had nodded and told him she would see, but no *mann* had asked to drive her home from service in over a year. No *mann* wanted a woman who could work as hard as he could. They wanted a cook and a cleaner, they wanted someone to bear them children, and Rose could never see herself doing any of those things.

The crying was replaced by laughter, as she knew it would be. Katie was a wonder with children. It was something that always mystified Rose. How did you stop a *boppli* from crying? How could you look after something so fragile and how did you have the patience to put up with so much crying? In all her years she had shied away from *kinner*. Animals were easy to live with... but *kinner*? They were difficult, awkward, and so vulnerable she could not bring herself to even think about having one. Maybe it was because of the hurt.

As she moved along the rows, she thought about the hurt look on her *daed's* face. How he wanted to see her happy and no matter how she tried she couldn't explain that she already was. There was no need for a husband in her life.

For many hours she had prayed on this. It didn't matter nothing came to her. There was no answer to her hurt. Nothing would make her trust. What if she married a *mann* and then changed her mind? What if he changed his mind? What if they had children and she let them down? If she betrayed them as her *mamm* had? No, it was too much to bear, she was much better off as she was. Like this, she could hurt no one. Here, she did her work and talked to *Gott,* her life was just as He wanted. She was sure of it. The loneliness was something everyone felt, she was sure of it.

Grab this wonderful Box Set now for FREE with Kindle Unlimited Amish of Faith's Creek 4 Book Box Set

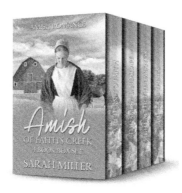

ALSO BY SARAH MILLER

All my books are FREE on Kindle Unlimited

If you love Amish Romance, the sweet, clean stories of Sarah
Miller you can receive free stories and join me for the latest
news on upcoming books here

These are some of my reader favorites:

The Amish Family and Faith Collection

Amish Baby Hope

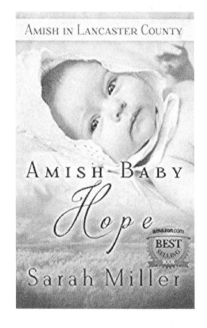

5 Amish Brothers Series

Find all Sarah's books on Amazon and click the yellow follow button

This book is dedicated to the wonderful Amish people and the faithful life that they live.

Go in peace, my friends.

As an independent author, Sarah relies on your support. If you enjoyed this book, please leave a review on Amazon or Goodreads.

ABOUT THE AUTHOR

Sarah Miller was born in Pennsylvania and spent her childhood close to the Amish people. Weekends were spent doing chores; quilting or eventually babysitting in the community. She grew up to love their culture and the simple lifestyle and had many Amish friends. The one thing that you can guarantee when you are near the Amish, Sarah believes is that you will feel close to God.

Many years later she married Martin who is the love of her life and moved to England. There she started to write stories about the Amish. Recently after a lot of persuasion from her best friend she has decided to publish her stories. They draw on inspiration from her relationship with the Amish and with God and she hopes you enjoy reading them as much as she did writing them. Many of the stories are based on true events but names have been changed and even though they are authentic at times artistic license has been used.

Sarah likes her stories simple and to hold a message and they help bring her closer to her faith. She currently lives in Yorkshire, England with her husband Martin and seven very spoiled chickens.

She would love to meet you on Facebook at https://www.facebook.com/SarahMillerBooks

Sarah hopes her stories will both entertain and inspire and she wishes that you go with God.